DEATH OF A FAT GOD
A **CRIME CLUB** *Novel*

A Crime Club Novel

The instant the elegant gold filigree doorknob clicked back into place the chief of police turned to her . . . The long and subtle chase was at its end.

" I have kept my promise."

He took one step towards her.

She put out her hand in a gesture which did not deny his claim but insisted on one more tiny delay.

But things are not quite what they seem at the start of this detective novel ; and later, when murder is committed on the stage of the Flinwich Opera House, they become extremely complicated and bizarre. For the singers who have come to perform at the Flinwich Festival have large temperaments as well as large voices, and cannot readily be diverted from the furious feuds and obsessive quarrels that are essential to their natures. To detect which of these exotic creatures has committed murder becomes the task of Superintendent Pryde of Scotland Yard C.I.D. Luckily, or unluckily, for him his work falls under the unsparing scrutiny of Mrs. Craggs, the charlady.

The Crime Club is proud to publish for the first time under its imprint the witty author of DEATH AND THE VISITING FIREMEN, ZEN THERE WAS MURDER and THE DOG IT WAS THAT DIED. DEATH OF A FAT GOD, with its informed and amusing glimpse of what goes on backstage in an opera house, will give pleasure to a large public and add to its author's growing reputation.

DEATH OF A FAT GOD

by

H. R. F. KEATING

Published for

THE CRIME CLUB

by COLLINS, 14 ST JAMES'S PLACE
LONDON

01590724

56336343

PT/PT

© H. R. F. KEATING, 1963
PRINTED IN GREAT BRITAIN
COLLINS CLEAR-TYPE PRESS : LONDON AND GLASGOW

CHAPTER I

THE DOUBLE DOORS closed softly together.
Discreetly. The instant the elegant gold filigree doorknob
clicked back into place the chief of police turned to her.

For a moment he made no other move. But the tensed
line of his arms, the involuntary slight thrust forward of
his head conveyed more clearly than words that he felt
that at last the time had come. The long and subtle chase
was at its end.

" I have kept my promise."

He took one step towards her.

She put out her left hand in a gesture which did not
deny his claim but insisted on one more tiny delay.

He looked at her questioningly. A lava flow of checked
rage and passion building up behind his intent eyes.

Quickly she put her last demand. The final clause in
the hard treaty they had fought out over the last intermin-
able half-hour.

A guarantee, in writing, signed by himself, allowing her
to go with the prisoner across the frontier.

He smiled slightly and with a faint inclination of the
head agreed to the request.

She stood watching him as he turned and walked across
to the heavily ornate desk. He moved, in spite of his
towering bulk, with quietness.

He sat down, seized a sheet of paper, snatched up the
pen and, without hesitation, began to write.

5

She relaxed a little.

Without turning round he asked which route she wanted to take.

" The shortest," she answered.

As if even to discuss this with him was more than she could bring herself to do.

He smiled again as he went back to his writing.

A fit of trembling came over her. Almost stumbling she went over to the supper table under the big uncurtained windows in search of the glass of wine he had offered her not long before. It was still standing where he had slid it towards her across the smooth surface of the heavy white linen cloth. With a half shake of her head she had contemptuously refused it then : now she caught hold of the frail goblet and lifted it, with her hand shaking, towards her mouth as if without its reviving effect and promise of a little oblivion she would fall senseless to the floor.

This was the glass he had taken up slowly and polished with a napkin after the prisoner had been dragged out of the room, exhausted and bleeding, to await the dawn and execution. When he had pushed the wine-filled goblet across towards her with all the oily finickiness of manner that characterised him, she had shot at him her last jet of contempt.

" Your price? " she had asked.

And imperturbably he had filled his own glass before naming it.

" How you hate me, and that is how I would have you."

Her head dropped forward at the thought of his words.

And there on the broad white cloth it lay. The knife.

Beside the plate with the apple on it, the flesh just turning brown where he had pared the long strip of peel away, there it lay. Small, but sharp. Deadly sharp.

The sudden realisation of what she could do went flooding through and over her.

She took one rapid glance behind her at the desk. The police chief was still sitting there, still writing. His great bulk seemed to dwarf the chair he sat on, turned at a slight angle to the desk. His thick neck was inclined forward so that the single slight crease across it was no longer visible. The light caught the short, blond hair, whose very colour seemed to add an unexpected extra of evil to the heavy menace of the brutal face.

With all the caution she could force herself to use she reached slowly across the table towards the apple plate. Still the police chief continued to write. She clasped the knife.

Scarcely daring to breathe she turned to face the desk, leaning against the supper table with her right hand just a little behind her so that the knife would be invisible to him.

He shifted slightly in his chair. There was a final noisy scratching from the pen. His signature. With calm, precise movements he folded the single sheet. Once, twice. He rose easily from the frail chair and turned towards her.

Now every last jot and tittle of their treaty was complete. Now nothing stood between him and what he had demanded.

He moved across the large, high-ceilinged room towards her, the safe-conduct held in his right hand, his arms extended.

" Mine. At last."

But the thickly voluptuous phrase was never finished. As the little sharp knife rose, flashed in the light for an instant, and plunged to the heart the words turned into a screaming curse.

Short, gasping, agonised.

She looked at him in a moment of steely triumph.

" *Questo è il bacio di Tosca.*"

Such is the kiss of Tosca.

Her harsh notes rang out in the resonant darkness of the hushed theatre.

The Scarpia staggered towards her, his arms making frenzied clutching movements.

She drew back, raising her arm in an attitude of terror.

Jean-Artaban Pivoine, who had not so long ago been acknowledged everywhere as one of the greatest Scarpias singing, performed his slow fall. The thud on the boards was heavier than it had been three or four years earlier, but an extra stone or more in weight is bound to tell.

Clarissa Glass took two paces forward to lean over the dying chief of police in triumph.

" *Muori dannato. Muori, muori, muori,*" she sang.

Die damned. Die, die, die.

Usually she found the hysterical passion too incomprehensible to deal with, but to-night she put more force into the curse than she had ever managed before. Had there been critics in the still silent audience they would have spoken more kindly of her Tosca than they had done on the opening night of the Flinwich Festival a week earlier. There would have been no remarks about it being a pity that one who had the physical presence for Tosca lacked the essential fire.

As the orchestra began the andante passage she walked back to the supper table keeping her eyes fixed on the recumbent body of the huge French bass-baritone. She tipped a little water on to one of the napkins and, rather perfunctorily, went through the motions of wiping the blood from her hand. Then she went over to the ornate mirror frame hanging sideways to the audience and stood in front of its blank surface pretending to straighten her hair.

Behind her back Jean-Artaban Pivoine slowly raised his right arm over his broad chest.

The gesture did not pass unnoticed in the audience. Jean-Artaban had made it very plain earlier that he was meant to be dead. But the people who attend the performances of opera bequeathed to the small industrial town of Flinwich by her most remarkable son, the millionaire, Simon Creassels, are not on the whole very knowledgeable. Some of them knew for certain that Scarpia should be dead, but the majority were prepared to believe that the plot dictated that Tosca's attempt on his life should fail. They sat in silence letting Puccini's chords roll sensuously over them.

Clarissa Glass gave her usual heavy start of surprise to denote that she had remembered the safe-conduct. She crossed to the desk as if to look for it. While she was making a show of going through the three or four pieces of paper provided by the property master Jean-Artaban rose to one elbow. He darted a look of malignant triumph in her direction and neatly fell back to the floor an instant before she turned to approach him.

He lay in perfect stillness as she pulled the folded sheet from his fingers.

Clarissa gave a sigh of relief that for once Jean-Artaban had not clutched at the safe-conduct with all the force of his big, pudgy fingers. He had done it at every performance so far, and she expected that to-night of all nights he would make things even more difficult for her. She thrust the folded sheet into the top of her dress as she rose.

" *E avanti a lui tremava tutta Roma*," she sang.

And before him trembled all Rome.

She noticed with slight surprise that this failed to get its usual reaction, but put it down to the fact that the aud.ence was no doubt following the plot even less than usual.

She turned and took her customary four paces towards the door.

Quickly Jean-Artaban raised his head just enough to attract attention. By the time Clarissa had checked herself at the sight of the two tall white candles on the little table by the door and had turned with them towards the candelabra on the supper table he was perfectly still again.

The orchestra quietly played the three chords of the Scarpia motive and Clarissa, looking more palely beautiful than ever, took the two lighted candles and placed them at the head and foot of the massive body of Jean-Artaban. She noted with pleasure that this time at least neither of them had flickered wildly and gone out.

She went for the crucifix hanging from a little hook at the wooden edge of one of the canvas flats.

Even in the few instants it took her to reach it down and turn round, Jean-Artaban had re-established communication with the audience.

Even those members of it who knew their *Tosca* were

keeping almost completely silent. It was difficult to know whether to draw in a sharp, shocked breath or to giggle frankly.

Clarissa laid the crucifix on Jean-Artaban's wide expanse of chest. Subconsciously she realised that he was breathing less heavily than he usually did at this stage, but she failed to draw any particular inference from this.

At the instant the timpanist began his low drum roll she turned and walked with bent head to the door. She had never been able to convey much emotion doing this, but in any case, she reckoned, the music was doing more than was needed.

Behind her Jean-Artaban reached for the crucifix with his right hand. He located it and holding it by the foot heaved himself up on his left elbow.

He was particularly pleased with the effect of tremendous effort he contrived to put into this.

Clarissa pushed open both leaves of the double doors.

Jean-Artaban swung himself sideways and on to his knees.

Clarissa went out and began closing the doors behind her. The music in the orchestra quietened to a pianissimo.

Quickly before the curtain swooped down Jean-Artaban got to his feet. He held the crucifix in front of him and with a single striking gesture laid Scarpia's curse on the departing Tosca.

CHAPTER II

" You go. You go."

With the steady roar of applause still audible on the far
side of the heavy curtain, Don Francisco de Zayas y
Tamago came striding on to the stage. Jean-Artaban was
standing stock still in the exact spot where he had launched
his curse, his enormous sides shaking with laughter.
With the back of the hand still holding the crucifix he
wiped tears of mirth from his eyes.

He appeared not to hear the sharply hysterical cries of
the Director of the Flinwich Festival. Certainly he took
no notice of them.

But Clarissa did hear. Together with the sound of Jean-
Artaban's laughter the words easily penetrated the thin
canvas of the flats. She turned and reopened the double
doors on to the stage.

As soon as Don Francisco saw her he pointed a thinly
elegant finger at the tall bulk of Jean-Artaban and
launched into full denunciation.

" I tell you : you go," he said. " Never in all my years
in the most great opera houses of Europe and the world
have I seen so disgraceful a behaviour. At La Scala they
would have shooted you. At Bayreuth they would have
put you on trial for treasons. At L'Opéra they would
have—have—— "

Words failed him and in a gesture of frenziedly eloquent
rage he indicated the terrible fate that would have been
meted out in Paris.

" At—at the Bolshoi," he began cascadingly again,

" they would have put you for life in solitary confinements. And—and at the Met they would have sue you. At Salzburg, at Salzburg—— "

But Jean-Artaban had turned round. From his towering height he looked down at the rigidly elegant form of the little Spaniard.

" How would you know what they would do? " he said. " They wouldn't let you one inch past the stage door at Salzburg. Or at the Met. Or at the Bolshoi. No, in Russia they wouldn't even let you set foot in the country. And if you sneaked your way in at Bayreuth or La Scala, they would throw you out by the seat of the pants. And as for L'Opéra, I will not mention L'Opéra in the same breath with you, you no-good know-nothing."

Don Francisco drew himself up to his full height. The curly black hair of his head came about level with the top of Jean-Artaban's chest. His eyes darted fire.

" But what the hell has happened? " Clarissa demanded. Neither of the others took the least notice of her.

" Listen to me," Don Francisco said.

His voice was as cold as the snows of the Pyrenees.

" Listen, if I had like I could have been director of any of these theatre. But there you can't do what you want. I won't consent to have my artistic freedom trammel. You know that, you know that about me. But look what happen at my seasons in Espain. You seen the cuttings. You—— "

" In Spain you can pay the journalists," said Jean-Artaban.

" No, no. It is not so. You lie. How you know? "

" What happened? What happened? Won't one of you tell me what all the damn' fuss is about? "

Clarissa's native Birmingham accent showed up more sharply when she had to shout.

By now the stage was beginning to get crowded with other singers, stage hands and members of the chorus. They had heard the beginning of the row and were anxious to follow its progress. Jean-Artaban was plainly delighted.

" I tell you how I know," he said, looking down urbanely at the fiercely trembling Spaniard. " I know because no journalist on earth would praise anything you did in the opera house without getting money for it. Plenty of money."

Don Francisco took three sharp steps backwards. He lifted his arm again and pointed full at Jean-Artaban's great fleshy face.

Like a gun.

" I say again : you go. You go now. I command you to go. You do not take the curtain callings. You never again appear in my theatre."

Clarissa darted into the space between Don Francisco's slight, rage-filled form and the looming bulk of Jean-Artaban.

" What happened? What happened? " she shouted.

Jean-Artaban smiled down from a tower of superiority.

" All right," he said to Don Francisco, again completely ignoring Clarissa, " all right, if I leave your lousy, stinking theatre, and your lousy stinking little English second-rate town for ever, how are you going to mount *Death of A Fat God*? "

He laughed, curtly.

" How are you going to mount *Death of A Fat God*? Tell me that."

Don Francisco's eyes redoubled their fire.

Smartly he jumped sideways so that the outrageously beautiful Clarissa no longer prevented him from directing his full batteries against Jean-Artaban.

"That is where you are wrong," he said. "That is where you make the most mistake of your life. The opera may be call *Death of A Fat God* but it isn't the Fat God that is difficult to cast. Any good bass can sing him. And they don't have to have plenty of natural fattiness on them. They are better with padding, a lot better. No, for this once, it is someone else who is the most necessary. We don't mount the opera for you. We mount her for Madame Da Costa-O'Brien. She is the one singer who can't be replace. You're the one who can. So, you go. You go. You go."

Jean-Artaban smiled.

He leant forward and patted the little Spaniard on the top of his head.

"I go," he said. "But you wait. You and I we are not finished yet."

He stalked majestically into the wings. For a moment he paused with the stage hands staggering past him taking off Scarpia's supper table and wheeling on the rostrum representing the battlements of the Castle of Sant' Angelo. He looked up at the row of dressing-rooms off the fly gallery which ran all round the back of the stage. Then a sudden secret smile gleamed in the corners of his eyes.

Instead of climbing the short flight of iron stairs which lead to the dressing-rooms and the fly gallery, he turned abruptly and hurried off in the direction of the gloomy stairway going down to the underparts of the stage.

His action went unnoticed.

Someone at last had told Clarissa what had happened behind her back and she was busy complaining about it to Don Francisco, who contented himself with saying alternately at intervals, " Yes, yes, he go " and " Calm yourself, think of your voice."

Meanwhile the battlements had almost assumed their right appearance. The cut-out silhouette of the Vatican and St. Peter's had been lowered into position and was being made fast. An assistant stage manager was putting the huge register of prisoners, the ink well and quill and the lantern on the sturdy little wooden table by the rough wooden stool ready for the Gaoler.

One of the company's music staff settled himself cautiously on the top of a tall, swaying pair of steps and peered through a pinpoint hole in the battlements to make sure that he could see the conductor and pass on his beat to the hidden contralto who was to sing the off-stage Shepherd Boy's song.

Suddenly the lighting changed from the dim interior of Scarpia's apartment in the Palazzo Farnese, in which the whole dispute between Don Francisco and Jean-Artaban had been conducted, into the cold blue starlit serenity of the hour before dawn out on the battlements.

Clarissa looked up at the sudden transformation. She turned and hurried away to her dressing-room in the gallery corresponding to the one on the other side of the stage where Jean-Artaban and the other male singers were accommodated. The comfort of a throat spray was urgently needed.

There was a flurry of last minute activity. The conductor was given his signal. He threaded his way out into the pit. From the far side of the curtain a brisk volley of applause could be heard.

The opening bars of the introduction to the last act began. The curtain went slowly up. The calm music rose and fell again into quietness. The tinkle of sheep bells superimposed itself. In the totally hushed theatre the creamy contralto of the Shepherd Boy floated into the hot darkness.

Right at the back of the stalls there was a large section of unsold seats even at the bargain prices which the generosity of the late Simon Creassels had ensured. In them sat the two theatre cleaners, Mrs. Craggs and Mrs. Milhorne. Mrs. Milhorne, who was still wearing her apron, rustled about among the sheets of the programme. At last she found what she wanted : a narrow slip of paper inserted among the pages. She peered at it from all angles but the darkness was too much for her.

She leant nearer Mrs. Craggs.

" Is this the one? " she asked.

Her whisper was penetrating.

Mrs. Craggs darted her a look of fury from under her flat, uncompromising, never discarded hat.

But when her friend Mrs. Milhorne got her teeth into something she was not easily deflected.

" Is this the one that's had to take over at the last minute? " she whispered again. " Because of the other one having that indisposition. I can't remember her name, if it is her."

In the darkness the Shepherd Boy's simple, sad air quietly rode over the orchestra. Mrs. Craggs decided that the quickest way to silence Mrs. Milhorne would be to tell her briefly what she wanted to know.

" Yes," she whispered back. " It is Margherita Clarone, and she did used to be Jean-Artaban Pivoine's wife."

" I thought so," said Mrs. Milhorne.

She nodded sagely and gave her attention to the music again. Against the faint glow of light coming from behind the curtained exit her head could be seen in silhouette, nodding nearly in time to the beat.

When the song was finished and as the grey, uncertain light of dawn was slowly spread over the castle battlements, Mrs. Milhorne turned to Mrs. Craggs again.

" Lovely," she said, " real lovely."

" Tone colour all wrong," said Mrs. Craggs.

She sniffed. In silence.

Mrs. Milhorne thought for a moment.

Then she leant nearer her friend.

" How do you know? " she asked. " It seemed really lovely to me. I don't see how you can know the lady was doing it wrong."

Mrs. Craggs did not attempt to deny Mrs. Milhorne her answer.

" I heard it often enough on the wireless," she said.

" Have you? " said Mrs. Milhorne. " Well, I know my old man wouldn't never consent to have opera on the radio. Can't stand all that screeching, he says. The sauce."

" There's got to be some compensations for being a widow," Mrs. Craggs whispered.

This provided Mrs. Milhorne with matter for thought. As Mrs. Craggs had intended.

" Yes, yes, I suppose there has," Mrs. Milhorne said.

She sank back into her own seat as the Gaoler came up through the stage trap and went across to light the lamp at the foot of the heavy crucifix hanging on one of the castle walls.

The opera took its course. The firing party arrived with the prisoner Cavaradossi. He was tactfully left by himself to sing " *E lucevan le stelle*." Clarissa came on escorted by Scarpia's minions. It was noticeable that her voice showed slight signs of wear from the fury of her denunciation of Jean-Artaban.

The mock execution took place without any hitch. Clarissa went through the motions of discovering that Cavaradossi was really dead after all and contrived a reasonable show of emotion. The exclamations of horror at the discovery of Scarpia's body came up loud and clear from beneath the stage. His minions duly rushed up through the trap and Clarissa made her customary vague pushing gesture, which as usual completely repulsed them.

She mounted the rostrum and turned to sing her cry to the ghost of Scarpia that they would meet before God preparatory to flinging herself, carefully, over the battlements. But even as she accurately hit the note on " *O Scarpia*," from the black square of the trap, up shot Scarpia himself, the triumphant Jean-Artaban.

Clarissa managed to complete her now meaningless phrase.

" . . . *avantia Dio*."

The orchestra crashed out its triple fortissimo.

Clarissa looked visibly doubtful about whether there was now any point in throwing herself to death. The conductor, sensing the disturbance, looked up from the orchestra to the stage. With notable presence of mind he held the last few bars as long as possible to give Clarissa a chance to come to a decision.

At last she shrugged a clear " It's quite beyond me " at the audience, turned and, even more perfunctorily than usual, flung herself over the battlements to kneel white with fury on the thick mat provided for her on the other side of the rostrum.

Jean-Artaban raised his arms high above his head. Almost certainly for the only time in the history of opera the story of Tosca had become the triumph of Scarpia.

The great curtain shot down like a guillotine descending to compensate Society for the monstrous crime committed against it.

This time Jean-Artaban did not wait to be attacked. As soon as the curtain had reached the stage he strode into the wings on the women's dressing-rooms side.

" Where is that creature? " he called out.

Don Francisco came rushing up.

" Quiet, quiet," he said in a voice which, high-pitched though it was, carried nearly as effectively as Jean-Artaban's.

The enormous Frenchman completely ignored him.

" Where is that creature? " he bellowed again. " Why was I not told she was here? I have forbidden her to sing in the same theatre with me. What is she doing here? "

Suddenly one of the dressing-room doors on the fly gallery in front of Jean-Artaban was flung open and a commanding figure wearing an elegant fur-trimmed suit stepped into the light.

" Well, Jean," she said in a rich, contralto voice, " do I hear you making a fuss as usual? "

" So it was you," Jean-Artaban said. " I knew it was. The moment I heard the first notes of the *pastore* song I recognised the voice. And, *mon Dieu*, how badly you sang it."

"Oh, so I sang badly? Well, that is as may be. But I sang the part I was engaged to sing. I didn't choose to come out on to the stage and try to steal the limelight with my little Shepherd Boy."

Jean-Artaban beckoned her towards him.

"Come down," he said. "Come down. Come down and I will give you what you deserve. I didn't hesitate to beat you when I was unfortunate enough to be married to you, I shall not hesitate to beat you now."

Margherita Clarone's dark eyes flashed.

"Not any more," she said. "I escaped from you once : I am not going to submit to your brutalities again."

Jean-Artaban took a step towards the iron stairway leading up to the gallery of dressing-rooms.

"If you so much as come near me I will call the police," his former wife said exultingly. "That will look very good in all the papers of the world, ' Famous Singer Sent To Prison '."

"Ah, yes," Jean-Artaban replied. "You are perfectly right. It will be in all the papers of the world. Jean-Artaban Pivoine, the bass-baritone with the most extra-ordinary range ever known, was put into prison for assault-ing a woman once believed to have been an opera singer."

But he made no further move to climb the stairs.

He had no need to.

His words had been as effective as any body blow.

Margherita Clarone went noticeably white. Her hands clutched the light iron railing of the balcony until it shook.

" Once believed to have been a singer," she said. " I, Margherita Clarone, once believed to have been a singer. You wait. You wait till you hear the applause for me as the Harpy in *Death of A Fat God* then you will know whether I am a singer or not. There is a role I can play, a role of passion, a role of fire. There is a role that will call up the depths in me. And you will hear them call for me at the curtains. ' *Bis, bis* ' they will cry. ' *Bis, bis,* where is the great Margherita Clarone? ' "

Jean-Artaban shook his great blond head sadly from side to side.

" *Ma pauvre petite,*" he said quietly. " I see you do not at all know our Flinwich audience. They do not cry ' *bis* ' : they cry ' encore.' But they do not even cry ' encore.' They know nothing of opera. They do not recognise a great voice when they hear it."

" Perhaps not," Margherita said, " but there is more to opera than a voice. You will never learn that, Jean-Artaban. You think you have only to go on stage and let fly with those great bull-frog notes for all the world to come to hear. But people want more than that : they want to be moved. They want great acting as well as great singing. And Flinwich will get that ; Margherita Clarone is here."

Suddenly Jean-Artaban whipped round and took two quick steps which brought him face to face with Don Francisco.

" Yes," he said, " Margherita Clarone is here. Why is that? You knew I have said she must not appear with me. That is known in every opera house in the world. And yet you dared to engage her. What is the meaning of it? "

" But—but—— " stammered Don Francisco.

Jean-Artaban did not interrupt. In chilling silence he waited for an explanation.

Don Francisco had not been able to stay the pace. He swallowed once or twice, and looked round him like a hunted man.

Still Jean-Artaban said nothing.

" Birgid Bjornsten has throat trouble," Don Francisco said at last.

" So that poor stupid Norwegian has not treated her throat properly. She has done too much work. I could have told her what would happen."

Don Francisco shrugged his thin shoulders.

" So we had to get someone else to sing the contralto part in *Death of A Fat God*," he said.

" And that explains why my former wife sang the Shepherd Boy to-night, I suppose. A likely tale."

" She had come down to discuss things with me," Don Francisco said. " We were going to explain everything to you."

A spurt of fire returned.

" Now that will not be necessary," he said. " Now you are going. Now I can produce the *Fat God* the way I want her. Now I shan't have to battle and fighting with a pig-head singer."

Into the word " singer " he put considerable contempt.

" I still do not know why I was affronted with the voice of that woman this evening," Jean-Artaban said.

" Little Gwynneth Davies caught a cold," Don Francisco said. " There was no one else near. There was no time to tell you. We had slips for the programme duplicating, and that was all."

" I see," said Jean-Artaban. " It was easy for you. She

was the first singer to hand. There are no such things as aeroplanes. You couldn't possibly have got one of the hundreds of contraltos there are in the world. No, you must have her. And I know why. You wanted to flaunt her in front of me. To insult me. To get rid of me."

"You got rid of yourself," Don Francisco snapped. "After making a farce out of *Tosca* you are finish."

"Ah, my friend, you have given yourself away. I know you : you are the great producer. You are the one who does not wish to have to listen to singers. You think opera is just an orchestra and puppets to move about on a stage, making them kneel and lie down and stand on their heads and all the while expecting them to sing like they had gramophone records in their stomachs. No wonder you wanted to get rid of Jean-Artaban Pivoine."

"I tell you I did not try to get rid of you, but I am glad I have. Opera would be the better thing if someone would get rid of you for ever. Singing, singing : that's all you thoughting about. Singing your head off and having the stupid people adore you for it."

"Yes," said Jean-Artaban, "people adore me : that is what you cannot endure. They are bored stiff with your clever productions and they adore my voice. There you have it. And you are so foolish as to try to get rid of me by bringing that woman here. You are so stupid as to try your little tricks when all the while you are making a great explosion for yourself. Do you not know that to put the two of us together is like putting together fire and dynamite. There will be a big bang, and someone will very likely be killed. And all to please you, you little——"

He searched for an epithet.

"You little producer."

" Yes, you are right there, Jean-Artaban," Margherita called down from her gallery. " You are right there. I am the fire, and I do not care how big is the explosion."

" No, no, no."

Don Francisco buried his head in his hands.

" Why must you always do it? " he said. " Opera is an art, the most great art. She is the fusion of all that is best in the human spirit under one guiding hand to make the effect that must be the most astonishing. And what happen? All the time there are quarrel and fightings and boastings. Why? Why? Why? "

" One guiding hand."

Jean-Artaban was quick to seize the point.

" One guiding hand of genius," he said. " Don Francisco de Zayas y Tamago directing his puppets. Look at him, the great master mind."

He took a step nearer the little erect figure of the Spaniard until the contrast in their heights was most apparent. It looked as if he had only to lean forward to blot out the little Spaniard entirely.

Don Francisco jumped back.

" Get out," he shouted. " Get out. No matter what you say, no matter what insults you bring, I am still master here. I, Don Francisco, am director of the Flinwich Festival. And I tell you, Jean-Artaban Pivoine, that you are no longer in my employ."

" In your employ? Do you think I am one of your servants? Let me tell you I know what it is to be a master. Have I not got my own château in France? Have I not got my own servants? My own butler? My own chauffeur? Have I not with the wonderful range of my voice earned myself a prince's fortune? Do you think I want to be

employed by you? No, thank you. You have asked me to
go. Very well. For now I go. But you wait and see what
happens. You wait."

CHAPTER III

JEAN-ARTABAN strode majestically round behind
the stage towards the men's dressing-rooms. Behind him
he left the small crowd who had collected to watch the
encounter with his stormy ex-wife divided in its attitudes.

There were, first, those who were quick to glory in
having witnessed a major row with their own eyes.
Opposed to them there was a large body who preferred to
pretend that they had become involved accidentally and
had not really heard most of what went on. Then each
of these two main parties was divided. Almost everybody
in both camps was against Jean-Artaban, but there was a
small section which busily announced its delight in the
sweep and viciousness of his attacks on Don Francisco and
Margherita. And Margherita herself divided the onlookers into two unequal bands. The larger was pas-
sionately in favour of her and loud in praise of her beauty
and fire. It was made up mostly of stagehands. The
opposition, mostly feminine, was very ready to decide that
if Jean-Artaban had left her she had certainly asked for it.

Don Francisco also divided opinion. In his case most
of the women present were extremely sympathetic. They
were joined in their commiseration by the more intellectual among the onlookers who greatly admired the
aristocratic little Spaniard's daring ways with production.

But a considerable knot of stagehands were only too ready to express their contempt, either on the grounds that Don Francisco never thought of the working-man or because they considered that he ought to have stood up more effectively to Jean-Artaban's bullying.

Among those who felt it important to establish that they had not deliberately eavesdropped on a private conversation was Mrs. Craggs's friend, Mrs. Milhorne. They had both come round backstage as soon as the performance was over so as to be ready to get into the dressing-rooms as soon as they were empty and start their task of cleaning them.

"Well," Mrs. Milhorne said, "if I'd known I was going to hear that sort of thing I wouldn't have been so keen to come round."

"If you don't get into them dressing-rooms as soon as you get a chance you're here all night," Mrs. Craggs said.

She had worked in the theatre for all the previous Flinwich Festivals and was concerned that Mrs. Milhorne, whose first experience of theatre work this was, should learn the ropes.

"But all the same," said Mrs. Milhorne, "such goings-on, I wouldn't have believed. I shouldn't wonder if old Simon Creassels isn't turning in his grave this moment."

"Not a bit of it," said Mrs. Craggs. "He knew what opera was like. Spent thousands on it in his time, and on entertaining the stars. It was all in the *Advertiser* a week or two back."

She put a wealth of meaning into the word "entertaining."

"Well," Mrs. Milhorne said, "I suppose he knew what he was about. But I don't like it. I got my feelings—

that's what my old mum used to say about me : ' Little Flo's got her feelings,' she used to say—and I don't like to hear all this violence. Talking about people being killed and everything. It isn't nice."

" 'Course it isn't nice," Mrs. Craggs said. " But it's the way they go on. So you'd better learn to like it, or else lump it."

" I'm sure I never thought that a man like old Mr. Creassels with all that money had anything to do with things like this," Mrs. Milhorne said.

She looked round with wide pale eyes at the backstage chaos.

Seen from behind, the rostrums and flats of the battlements of the Castle of Sant' Angelo presented a dingy and haphazard appearance. Parts of other settings for the opera, detached from their proper surroundings, had a disturbing air of grotesque forlornness. Baron Scarpia's supper table stood where it had been pushed higgledy-piggledy by the stagehands clearing away the furniture of the previous act. One of the people who had stopped on their way out to watch the battle between Jean-Artaban and Don Francisco had dumped a large battered suitcase among the richly gilt cutlery and sparkling goblets.

Here and there stood little clumps of other properties— a painter's easel with a showy portrait of the Marchesa Attavanti on it, a basket full of mysterious parcels, a lavish bouquet of artificial flowers. Lacing the whole fantastic backstage jumble together was a mass of ropes strung tautly in all directions in a web of complexity too elaborate for the eye to follow.

" He was a respectable gentleman was old Mr. Creassels," Mrs. Milhorne said.

It was plain that the wild confusion of the opera house was in her eyes far removed from respectability.

"Respectable," said Mrs. Craggs. "He wasn't respectable : he was rich."

Mrs. Milhorne made a faint gesture of protest.

"Old Mr. Creassels was pretty well ripe for the loony bin," Mrs. Craggs went on. "If he hadn't been so well off I dare say they'd have tucked him away long before he died."

"Well," Mrs. Milhorne admitted, "it certainly does seem a bit strange like to make such a fuss about all this."

Again she darted a look at the criss-cross of ropes, the snaking tangle of cables and the mad jumble of properties and scenery.

"I don't know much about that," Mrs. Craggs said. "You got to have this—— "

She jerked a contemptuous thumb in the direction of Scarpia's supper and the battered suitcase.

" ——so's you can have that."

She indicated with a nod of her square hat the front part of the stage, still the monumental and tragic battlements of Sant' Angelo.

"But all the same," she went on, "perhaps you have got to be a bit touched to spend so much on it all. And there was other things funny about him, too. If he was a bit crazy over singers, he was just as crazy the other way round about lawyers. Couldn't abide the sight of a lawyer, high or low. And they're only ordinary folk, stands to reason."

"Yes, I suppose so," said Mrs. Milhorne.

She sounded doubtful.

"I was asked to give evidence in a police-court case

once," she added after a pause. " 'Course I wouldn't do it. Me, go into one of them places. I'd have fainted right away on the spot."

Mrs. Craggs sniffed.

Suddenly she turned and looked up.

Jean-Artaban had stayed in his dressing-room only long enough to wrap himself in a huge fur-collared overcoat, radiating opulence from every fibre. The mild chill of the early autumn evening scarcely called for a coat which, so gossip in the opera houses ran, had first served as Colline's famed garment in *La Bohème*. But Jean-Artaban was well known for flaunting it at any conceivable opportunity.

With his theatrical make-up still on his face, he strolled ostentatiously down the iron stairs from the fly gallery and across towards the corridor which led to the stage door.

The crowd who had collected to watch his outburst over Margherita had not had time or inclination to disperse. All eyes watched him as he slowly paraded his way out.

From the gallery opposite, Margherita, still standing looking down at the stage, gave a toss of her dark head. Don Francisco, who had been searching for someone sympathetic to pour out his troubles to, turned deliberately away.

Jean-Artaban, plainly conscious of the hush his re-appearance had brought, went slowly and smilingly towards the stage door.

He was not to leave the theatre on this effective note.

Hardly had he got to the corridor leading to the stage door when he stopped abruptly. A slightly sheepish look crept over his face.

The transformation was so sudden that almost everybody noticed it. There was a good deal of craning of necks to see who or what it was in the corridor that had produced so startling a change. One or two of the more openly curious walked over to positions where they could see for themselves.

A little dumpy woman of about sixty was standing in the small lobby by the stage doorkeeper's box. Her hair was blued and cut by a master, she wore a discreet mask of cosmetics, her open mink coat showed a suit evidently cut by a tailor of distinction. And none of it helped.

She might as well have left her hair its natural grey, not bothered with make-up and worn something off the peg. Nothing could have altered the simple ordinariness of her appearance.

Mrs. Craggs had not been one of those to move to see who had so transformed the arrogant Jean-Artaban. But luckily for Mrs. Milhorne, who was exuding curiosity from every angle of her skimpy frame, they were both standing in a position to get first look at the newcomer.

" Why," said Mrs. Craggs, " that must have surprised Jean-Artaban. I happened to hear him saying earlier this evening that she was safely tucked away in London."

" Who is it? " whispered Mrs. Milhorne.

She rose up on wobbling tiptoe with excitement.

" It's Madame Pivoine, dear," said Mrs. Craggs. " Haven't you ever seen her picture in the papers? "

" I can't say as I have. Is she another of them singers? She don't look it."

" Singer."

Mrs. Craggs was contemptuous.

" She's no singer. She's a millionairess, American, of course. One of the Towell girls that was. The only one of 'em left now. Alice Towell Pivoine she calls herself, now she's married to him."

"Been married before then, has she?" asked Mrs. Milhorne.

"Don't you never read the papers?"

Mrs. Milhorne tossed her narrow head.

"I don't much care for all that gossip," she said. "It's crude if you ask me."

"It's only human nature," said Mrs. Craggs grimly. "And anyhow if you had read it you'd have known. She ain't never been married before, not that one."

Alice Towell Pivoine saw her husband at almost the same moment that he saw her.

She took a quick look up and down him.

"Why, Jean-Artaban," she said, "I guess I should never have stayed up in London."

Jean-Artaban recovered his presence of mind.

"Alice, my own Alice," he said.

There was no difficulty in hearing him even at the other side of the big stage.

Margherita pricked up her ears and moved quickly but quietly along the gallery until she had a clear view of the stage-door corridor.

Jean-Artaban swept forward, lowered his immense bulk forward from the waist, took his wife's stubby little hand and with the utmost gallantry kissed it.

"Thank you, dear," she said.

"But, my own one, why have you so suddenly arrived here out of the night?" Jean-Artaban said.

Alice smiled.

"I guess I must have had a premonition about you, Jean-Artaban," she answered.

Jean-Artaban did not pursue this line of inquiry.

"But how did you get here? Are you cold? Have you had something to eat? Why not come back to the hotel with me *tout de suite*?"

The air was a-flutter with solicitude.

Alice put up her hand to quieten him down.

"Now I've looked after myself quite well," she said. "After all, I did it for years before I met you and I'm perfectly capable of doing it again."

"But you shall not. I, Jean-Artaban Pivoine, forbid it. No longer will you have to fight with all these things for yourself. That is why I married you, to look after you properly, not to let you be exposed to the harshnesses and cruelties of the so cold world."

Alice Towell Pivoine put her head a little on one side like an intelligent, well-fed sparrow and contemplated her enormous husband.

"Now, Jean-Artaban, you know perfectly well that the world has never been exactly so cold for me. It's just amazing what people will do for money."

Jean-Artaban spread his great hands wide.

"Ah, for money," he said. "Yes, for money people will do things. But they will do them without love. And it is with love that your poor old Jean-Artaban does things for you, my sweet one."

Alice looked pleased, but not entirely deceived.

"Well," she said, "we'll just forget about whatever it is you have done. If it's too truly appalling I dare say I'll get to hear of it sooner or later. Now, tell me how it went to-night."

Jean-Artaban's immensely broad back could be seen to quiver.

" To-night? " he said.

" Why, yes. How did your Scarpia go? Did you manage ' *Gia mi dicon venal* ' all right? "

Jean-Artaban drew himself up to his full height.

" When have I ever been known to fail with it? " he said. " No Scarpia in the world can do it justice the way I do."

" Well, yes, dear, but you know you had to take an extra breath at the last performance at the San Carlo."

" Bah. That was nothing. A touch of a cold. What else could it be? "

" It could be that you're getting to the age where you have to think about your voice more. You can't expect to be able to sing everything with scarcely any rehearsal for ever."

The great blond head dropped forward.

"Ah, my little one, you are so good for your wicked Jean-Artaban. What would he do without you? Without someone to tell him, every now and again, the truth? That is what I have always missed in all the years of my wanderings. That is what you mean to me."

" Well, you always did know how to make a pretty speech, I'll say that for you. And now, let's get away to the hotel. I expect you're hungry as usual, and I could do with a mite to eat myself."

Jean-Artaban flicked his hand in the air as if he was summoning all the carriages in Europe.

" Then let us go."

" But just a word first with Don Francisco. He'd be so hurt if he thought I'd called in and not said hallo."

" But there is no need."

" Oh, but I think there is. I see a lot of people on the stage. Someone's bound to tell him I was here."

" Let them tell him. You do not have to make obeisance to him every time you enter the Flinwich opera house."

Alice smiled up at him.

" Well, of course I don't, dear. But all the same it would be only polite. And I never heard yet that I'd forgotten my manners."

" But he may not be there."

" If he isn't, there's no harm done."

Alice walked forward. For a moment it looked as if Jean-Artaban was not going to move his enormous body which effectively blocked the wide corridor. But Alice had taken only two steps when he moved aside and with an inclination of the head let her pass.

He followed her like a giant hangdog spaniel as she came down the corridor and out into the cluttered backstage chaos. She spotted Don Francisco at once and sailed over to him with a twinkling smile.

Don Francisco looked caught on the wrong foot.

" Hallo there," said Alice Towell Pivoine. " I'm only just passing by, but I had to have a look around and see if you were anywhere about."

Don Francisco's temperature dropped visibly.

He clicked his heels together and bowed his curly black head over Alice's hand.

" We are always delighted to see you, madame," he said.

There was only the slightest emphasis on the " you."

" Well, Don Francisco," Alice said, " that goes for me, too. I just love coming round backstage at the opera. I guess it gives me a real romantic thrill."

She glanced up and round at the weaving, crossing ropes, the looming flats and the confusion of rich and glittering properties. Then she looked sharply at the immense and forlorn figure of her husband.

"Though I do sometimes find the Pivoine family is not as welcome as it might be," she said.

The quick, shrewd look she darted at Don Francisco made him blush openly.

But he managed a magnificently vague wave of the hand, dismissing for all time whatever little clouds might ever have appeared on any possible horizon. And specifying nothing.

Alice Towell Pivoine was not a person to specify things in front of. There was an almost palpable sense of general relief at Don Francisco's tactful silence.

"A voice like Jean-Artaban's makes her own welcome in every opera house in the world," he said.

"That's real pretty," said Jean-Artaban's wife.

She turned to her towering spouse.

"Now, honey," she said, "I guess we mustn't stay taking up Don Francisco's time any more. I know a director's day is never done."

Jean-Artaban breathed a prodigious sigh of relief and bowed solemnly in the approximate direction of Don Francisco.

He turned to escort his wife away.

It was plain that embarrassing questions of future performances were to be discussed through the polite medium of the post.

But Alice Towell Pivoine's peace of mind was not to be preserved so easily.

A clatter of high heels on the iron stairs leading from

the women's dressing-rooms side of the fly gallery made Jean-Artaban turn his head.

It was Margherita.

"Jean-Artaban, Jean-Artaban," she called out as he quickly turned away again.

Jean-Artaban bent solicitously over the warmly clad form of his present wife.

"Come, my little one," he said, "we will soon have you back safely in the hotel after the *froidure* of this night."

He ought to have known that his wife could not be handled like this.

She stopped and turned.

From the foot of the iron stairway Margherita advanced.

Regally.

Alice looked at her. Nothing in her features showed her feelings.

Poker face.

"Ah, Jean-Artaban," Margherita said, "this is a moment I have long waited for. Won't you introduce me to your new wife?"

"Margherita."

Jean-Artaban burst into rage like a rocket leaving the launching pad.

But he was interrupted.

Alice stepped forward holding out her hand.

"Margherita Clarone," she said. "I don't need any introduction to you. I've seen you often enough on the stage, and heard you and admired you."

Margherita melted.

"You are too kind," she murmured.

" Why, no," said Alice. " No one could help admiring that lovely contralto of yours. There's nowhere else we can hear a voice of such fire."

Margherita gestured the compliment aside.

" It is a magnificent voice," she acknowledged.

" And I'm delighted to have met its owner," said Alice. She paused fractionally.

" If that's the right word," she added.

But qualifications were lost on Margherita.

She stepped forward and kissed Alice on both cheeks.

" It is right that we should be friends," she said. " We have waited too long."

Warmly she slipped her arm through Alice's and set off with her in the direction of the stage door.

Jean-Artaban looked baffled. Temporarily.

" After all," Margherita added with a shrug, " we have a lot of problems in common."

She flicked a glance behind her in the direction of her ex-husband.

" Well," said Alice without looking back, " I'm only indirectly concerned in all this opera business, you know. I don't have to worry about the problems in the way you and Jean-Artaban do. You know, I had no idea before I married him of all the troubles you singers have to put up with, not talking too much before a performance, not staying up too late nights, not drinking too much, cutting down on smoking, keeping out of the hot sun. I had just no idea you had such difficult lives."

They had almost reached the stage door.

Alice turned to Margherita again.

" Well, dear," she said, " it's been a pleasure to meet you, and I only hope we see a lot more of each other now the ice is broken. But I know you must be anxious to get back to your hotel and get a good night's sleep, so I won't keep you any more, much as I'd like to."

She slid her arm dexterously out of Margherita's and would have swept out into the night had not Margherita, with a silvery laugh, held her lightly, but implacably, by the shoulder.

" Good-night, my dear," she said. " And you take our big troublesome bear away and see that he gets an early night. I thought this evening that his voice is showing a little the strain."

" But, no."

This was the limit of Jean-Artaban's protest. But there was outrage in both syllables.

" I think that is why he was a bit naughty to-night, too," Margherita added.

Don Francisco, who had been hovering in the background like a tactful head waiter, jumped forward.

" Margherita," he said. " Margherita, I—I— I —— "

A flash of inspiration.

He turned to Alice.

" You will excusing me, dear lady," he said, " but to-morrow we begin the rehearsings for *Death of A Fat God*, so it is the most necessary that I speak with Signorina Clarone."

" But, of course," said Alice.

Margherita turned a fiery smile on the slight form of Don Francisco.

" In a moment, in a moment," she said. " Just now Jean-Artaban's wife and his ex-wife are talking about their great naughty little boy."

But while Margherita's attention had been momentarily

directed towards the harassed little Spaniard Alice had contrived once more to slip from her grip. Now she raised a deprecating hand.

" Ah," she said, " we've both of us a great deal to say on that subject, I'm sure. Far, far too much for one night. No, we'll meet again, my dear."

She actually got out into the glittering starlit October night. But Margherita was not beaten yet.

She flung both arms up in a gesture of despair.

" Oh," she said, " if we were to go through the whole catalogue . . . I could see at once to-night that he has not changed."

She turned to the enormous, blond bass-baritone.

" No, Jean-Artaban, to-night I think you excelled yourself."

Don Francisco, almost crouching to the ground, wriggled himself between her and the Pivoines.

" Excelled yourself, my dear friend," he said to Jean-Artaban. " Certainly you are excelling yourself. Never have I heard the voice so magnificent."

Jean-Artaban had the grace to bow.

Margherita was for the moment nonplussed.

And a moment was all Jean-Artaban needed. Almost lifting his dumpy wife into the air he bundled her into the huge shiny car which was waiting for them in the dingy back street which the stage door gave on to. In a flash he had placed his own enormous bulk between her and the tell-tale Margherita.

He must have realised at once that he had saved the situation. His spirits palpably soared. He leant his massive head out of the car window.

" Good-night. Good-night, Don Francisco, my dear friend," he said. " And I shall not forget what you have said. Nothing that you have said to-night will I forget."

CHAPTER IV

AT THE EARNEST request of Mrs. Milhorne, Mrs. Craggs consented next morning to prolong their spell of cleaning the bars and foyer until after the rehearsals had begun so that they could have some work to do in the auditorium when the singers were on stage.

" It's not worth it, dear," Mrs. Craggs said. " They won't be singing proper, you know. Only sort of la-la-la-ing through. It's the first rehearsal on the stage."

" No, but all the same," Mrs. Milhorne said, " fancy seeing them at it."

Mrs. Craggs shrugged.

" I wouldn't cross the street to see you baking a cake, dear," she said. " Though if you was to offer me a slice of your cut-and-come-again I'd never say no."

" Well, I do bake 'em a treat," Mrs. Milhorne said.

But she was far away.

As they went out into the auditorium she spoke again.

" I think I might have made a lovely opera singer if it wasn't for keeping in tune," she said.

Mrs. Craggs was saved from deciding whether she had been meant to hear this or not by the arrival on the empty stage of Don Francisco.

He looked sharply round and glanced at his watch.

The two cleaners leaning on their brooms in the shadows of the unlit auditorium escaped his attention.

He muttered a sharp expression in Spanish and Mrs. Milhorne looked at Mrs. Craggs. Temperament already and the day hardly begun.

Don Francisco was going back into the wings on bouncing toes when a tall man of about thirty-five with a fattish face devoid of expression mooched out of the rococo door of Pasha Selim's house in the partly erected set for that evening's performance of *Il Seraglio*.

" Ah."

Don Francisco pounced on him.

" Where is everybodies? " he snapped. " For ten o'clock the rehearsings was called. Already it is after that. If there is no disciplining there is no art. Is that not so? "

" I suppose that you are right."

The tall young man looked round despondently and sat down on the edge of a low wall bounding the Pasha's garden. His shoulders drooped and his head fell forward till it was almost on his knees.

" I am afraid that is so," he murmured.

A trace of French accent was noticeable in his voice.

Don Francisco looked at him. He gave an explosive shrug of his shoulders and went off again in the direction of the stage door.

But evidently he found no one because within a few seconds he was back.

" Nobody coming, nobody coming," he spluttered.

He looked at the heap of person on the low wall.

" You," he said, " you I was not expect. After I tell your father he go I was not expect you to come to-day."

Jean-Artaban Pivoine's son raised his pale wide-cheeked face.

"My father is coming," he said. "But you know he is always late for rehearsal. He is driving round Flinwich waiting till he is sure everybody is here. He said to me when he called me in to see him this morning, 'Paul, I wish you to be at the theatre exactly on time to give that Don Francisco something to think about'."

He looked up at the little Spaniard with a forlorn, half-pleading air.

"Please, don't tell him I was not here exactly at ten," he said.

Don Francisco pursed his lips.

"So," he said, "he try to give me something to think about, is it? I give him something if he set feet in this theatre. I give him a policeman to think about."

Paul Pivoine looked up again for a moment.

"I—I don't think. . . ." he said.

But putting advice before the ebullient little Spaniard turned out to be beyond his capabilities.

His head sank again.

"Well, in any case, since you are here you will play for us," Don Francisco said. "It will be easier than I myself play."

Paul Pivoine got up without a word and began shambling off in the direction of the tunnel leading to the orchestra pit where the elderly upright rehearsal piano stood.

Only when he had slumped on to the piano stool did he speak.

"My father said I was to play."

" It is not your father. It is I——— "

But Don Francisco was interrupted by the arrival of the main body of the cast for *Death of A Fat God*.

They were led by Madame Da Costa-O'Brien. Madame Da Costa-O'Brien would not have consented to walk on to the stage of any opera house other than at the head of any group whatever, especially a group of singers. She was a magnificent body of a woman. Almost six feet tall, barrel-chested, bull-shouldered, elephant-hipped. Her dress of heavy brocaded material hung heavily down to well below her knees. Her hair, which was of a peculiar metallic blackness, was set in majestic coils. Here and there ancient Celtic ornaments were embedded in it.

Down in the darkness of the auditorium Mrs. Milhorne immediately recognised her as a personality.

" Who is it? " she whispered to Mrs. Craggs.

The " it " seemed natural and appropriate.

But when Mrs. Craggs repeated the name Mrs. Milhorne plainly needed more enlightenment.

" She's the great soprano," Mrs. Craggs said. " That's why they're doing this Prokovinski opera. She's the only person in the world who could possibly sing the heroine."

Mrs. Milhorne blinked at the statuesque form of the great diva.

" What is the heroine then? " she said. " Some sort of goddess or other, I suppose. Unless it's one of them soldier-ladies, Amazons I think they call them."

" She's a goose girl as a matter of fact," said Mrs. Craggs.

She sounded embarrassed.

Mrs. Milhorne put her long, pale face on one side and

scrutinised Madame Da Costa-O'Brien at greater length.

" What sort of a goose girl? " she asked.

" Just a goose girl," Mrs. Craggs replied. " Don't ask me all about it. I only know what I've been told. That young Monsieur Pivoine was talking to me about it the other day."

Mrs. Milhorne turned her attention to the slumped figure on the piano stool in the orchestra pit.

" 'Im," she said.

" He's the only one of 'em you can always be sure of a friendly word out of," Mrs. Craggs said.

But Mrs. Milhorne was looking at Madame Da Costa-O'Brien again.

In wonder.

" 'Course," said Mrs. Craggs, " I don't say but what he ought to stick up for himself a bit more than he does, but it makes a relief in a place like this all the same."

" No," said Mrs. Milhorne slowly. " Did he tell you more about what sort of a goose girl she was meant to be? "

" He may have mentioned something."

Mrs. Craggs took a duster from the pocket of her flowered apron and went over and flicked at the top of a fire extinguisher. She looked at the heavy grime which had come off on the duster and sighed.

" Well, what did he say? "

Mrs. Milhorne had followed her.

Mrs. Craggs turned towards her friend.

" He said she's described by the tenor as a wisp of cloud, bright promise of a day renewed."

She spoke bitterly.

It made things difficult when the more intractable aspects of the art she loved would present themselves so insistently to the view.

" But you should hear her sing," she added.

Mrs. Milhorne shook her lank head slowly from side to side.

" I dunno," she said, " perhaps I was a fool to give up the municipal offices job after all."

On the stage there had been a great deal of handshaking and good mornings in several languages. For a little while all had been animation and vivacity. Madame Da Costa-O'Brien had inclined her head and had made some forthright comments about the weather. But quite suddenly the supply of small talk had come to an end.

Don Francisco looked round about him with great care.

" I think we can beginning," he said. " As you will all knowing Jean-Artaban will not after all sing the part of the god. But already I have spoken on the telephone with Michael Miller in New York and it is almost arranged that he fly over to taking the part. He is learn it to-day. And for just now we do not need . . ."

His voice trailed away.

It had been borne in on him that no one was paying any attention.

He tried to peer over Madame Da Costa-O'Brien's shoulders at what appeared to be the source of the distraction away in the wings. But it would have taken a man a good deal taller than Don Francisco to peer over Madame Da Costa-O'Brien's shoulders.

No one seemed put out that Don Francisco had failed to complete his sentence and so he was forced to go to the edge of the little semi-circle of singers who had gathered to listen to him and to dodge round to see what the trouble was.

His short erect back shook convulsively.

" No," he said.

His shout, though squeaky, was so loud that he once more gained attention. The group gave way.

Don Francisco was left in isolation to confront the portly towering form of Jean-Artaban Pivoine, once a principal bass-baritone of the Paris Opéra.

" No," Don Francisco said again.

This time he hit a lower note.

Jean-Artaban smiled. Like a giant lizard.

" You must go out," Don Francisco said. " Go out or I send for the polices."

Jean-Artaban gave a tiny shrug of his vast shoulders.

" But I am singing here," he said. " I am taking the part of the god in Prokovinski's *Death of A Fat God*. The rehearsal has been called for ten o'clock this morning."

He glanced airily round.

" I do not exactly know what is the time," he said, " but I expect it is a few minutes before ten. I am here. I am ready."

" You are not singing the part of the god in Proko-vinski's *Death of A Fat God*," said Don Francisco. " You are not taking any part more in the Flinwich Festival. Last night you were dismissaled for the most great contempt of the director and for making come to life again Scarpia."

" Ah," said Jean-Artaban, " you wish to keep to your hasty words, yes? "

" Yes. *Si. Oui.*"

Jean-Artaban grinned.

" That is excellent," he said. " Because I remind you I have a contract."

Don Francisco drew himself up to his full height. The top of his curly black head came just underneath Jean-Artaban's lowest chin.

" The contract is teared up," Don Francisco said with dignity.

" Is teared up your copy," Jean-Artaban replied. " Is with the lawyers my copy."

He squared his wide and slightly flabby shoulders.

" I sue."

" Sue then."

Suddenly Jean-Artaban relaxed. He brought his great fat-cheeked face down to within a few inches of Don Francisco's.

" You are aware, I suppose," he said, " of the complete terms of the will of the late Mr. Creassels of this town? "

Don Francisco looked at him with contenpt.

" Of course."

Slowly Jean-Artaban smiled.

" Then you will know, without doubt, of the clause which says that because of the testator's great hatred of the law and all lawyers if the Director of the Flinwich Festival becomes engaged in any litigation whether of his own will or not he loses automatically his post? "

It took an appreciable amount of time for Don Francisco to absorb the meaning of the English.

But when he had done so, he went white.

He gulped twice.

Jean-Artaban turned away.

" But you would prefer to keep your honour and lose the directorship? " he said.

The remark carelessly tossed over his shoulder.

Everybody was looking at the little Spaniard.

He swallowed.

"Jean-Artaban," he said.

His voice was a croak.

"Jean-Artaban, I cannot bear to seeing you go like this. We are the most great old friends. You must come back."

Jean-Artaban turned round.

"You are asking me back?" he said.

"Yes, yes, my old friend, I am asking you back."

"You withdraw your dismissal?"

Don Francisco bowed.

"I withdraw it completely."

"You apologise for insulting my artistic integrity?"

"I apologise."

"With humbleness?"

"With humbleness."

No one was looking at Don Francisco any longer. Everyone was looking at their feet or into the far distance.

"That is excellent," said Jean-Artaban.

His voice was slopping over with self-satisfaction.

"Now," he added, "as I have arrived early we will begin the rehearsal from my entrance in the last act, and you can go back to the beginning afterwards. In that way I will be spared the ordeal of listening to Don Francisco's reflections on the art of Prokovinski. So, commence."

But a question of precedence had arisen.

Madame Da Costa-O'Brien, who had been conducting a close examination of the artificial figs on the fig-tree in the Pasha Selim's garden, revolved.

"Excuse me," she said.

Her voice was regality and ice.

" Did I hear some question being discussed of where the rehearsal should start? "

Don Francisco came across towards the fig-tree, interrupting himself after every second pace for a quick, nervous bow.

" I think, madame, you may not have had the pleasure of meeting Monsieur Pivoine? " he said.

He smiled ingratiatingly.

Madame Da Costa-O'Brien bowed her metallic black head very slightly in the direction of Jean-Artaban.

" No," she said, " we have not met."

She looked across at the bear-shaped form of the French bass-baritone.

" I believe you have not sung at the Metropolitan? " she said.

Jean-Artaban grew in stature.

" I have not sung at the Metropolitan? I, I have sung there. Perhaps the terms they have offered have not always been altogether pleasing to me. But I have thought it my duty at least once to sing in New York."

He shrugged.

" Even in America they are entitled to some art," he said.

Don Francisco turned and bowed hastily to Jean-Artaban.

" In Europe," he said, " Monsieur Pivoine has sung with great success in every major opera house."

" That is so," said Jean-Artaban.

" I have not found it convenient to come to Europe for a good many years," said Madame Da Costa-O'Brien.

" That has been our loss," Don Francisco said.

He brightened a little.

"Now happily repaired," he added. "And let me say now, madame, at the beginnings of our confrontation of Prokovinski's great work that it is to me a dreaming come true that you should have consent to sing a part which you, and you only, can undertaking. And it is a great pleasure that I have been able to make a gatheration of such artists to sing with you."

He bowed again to Jean-Artaban.

Madame Da Costa-O'Brien swept down from the fig-tree to the centre of the stage.

"Let me say how very pleased we are to be singing for you," she said. "And that I am sure that the singers which our good friend, Don Francisco, has drawn together to accompany us will be worthy of the task of interpreting this great opera."

At the dim back of the theatre Mrs. Milhorne shook her head.

"A wisp of cloud," she said.

"And now," Madame Da Costa-O'Brien added, "we will begin with the duet from Act I. We find it best to start with the heart of the matter."

She turned to the group of singers.

"Are you ready, Franz, my old friend?" she said.

A tubby, rather short man, who had been standing abstractedly humming to himself, stepped briskly forward. He took Madame Da Costa-O'Brien's hand in his, clicked his heels together with a noise like a pistol shot, bent like a jack-knife from the waist and kissed the diva's plump, ring-encrusted fingers.

"*Jawohl, gnae Frau,*" he said.

"Oh," said Mrs. Milhorne.

The syllable conveyed much. Surprise, rapture, disappointment.

" Is that really him? " she asked Mrs. Craggs. " Is that really Franz Prahler? "

" 'Course it's him," said Mrs. Craggs.

" He doesn't look like on the pictures," Mrs. Milhorne said.

" Hasn't got his blocked shoes on to-day, I dare say," said Mrs. Craggs. " And then they can't put him on a little platform for opera rehearsals, same as they does when he has to kiss the girl in the films."

" All the same," Mrs. Milhorne said, " I liked the way he kissed her hand like that just now, real romantic."

She brought herself to look at Madame Da Costa-O'Brien once more.

" The bright day renewed," she said. " I dunno. I really dunno."

" Madame."

The anguished plea came from Don Francisco.

" Madame, if you will excuse me. There are some observatings before the rehearsing begin."

He jumped up on the low wall of the Pasha's garden.

" Igor Dimitri Prokovinski," he said, " was, I must asking you all to remember, above all a Russian. So it is the Russian souling that to-day we—— "

" Yes, yes, my dear friend," Madame Da Costa-O'Brien broke in with a stately waving-down gesture, " but all that will keep till after we have sung. If anyone should wish to know what lies at the deep core of this opera, I suggest they simply listen."

" They will not in any case be able to help doing that," said Franz Prahler.

He stood stockily preening himself.

Madame Da Costa-O'Brien peered forward into the orchestra pit.

"Are you ready, young man?" she said. "Start from the beginning of No. 7. Or, no. There is a lot of prelude from the orchestra. We shan't need that. Begin about thirty bars in. Just before our entry."

Down in the pit Paul Pivoine obediently rustled the pages of his score. Then he began to play.

He crouched on the piano stool, which because of his tall frame was a good deal too high for him, and concentrated on the score in front of him with a nervous intensity frightening to watch. He managed to play the notes without ever exactly stumbling, but without ever conveying that he was at all happy in what he was doing.

Madame Da Costa-O'Brien took a tiny lace handkerchief out of her sleeve and cleared her throat with dreadful efficiency into it. Then she turned her eyes up to heaven.

Without actually coming to a full stop Paul Pivoine reached the point in the music where the duet started.

Madame Da Costa-O'Brien began to sing.

Immediately the cold theatre was transformed. Soaring into the chill half-darkness her translucent silver voice held every particle of attention. It was a made thing. Right beyond doubt, exact as machine-tooled steel, supremely beautiful.

It mounted, hung poised, descended. Each note was held to the exact instant, each was hit cleanly and truly as a hammer falling on its allotted place. And, more wonderful than anything, the voice was young. A wisp of cloud was singing. High and difficult though the music was, it was coming from the spirit of bright day renewed.

Then her song was taken up by Franz Prahler. His infinitely lyrical, golden voice blended and intertwined with the high, pure silver of the great soprano's.

Mrs. Craggs stole a glance at Mrs. Milhorne from under her intransigent hat.

Mrs. Milhorne's mouth was hanging open. Her lank face was lit up by a rare radiance. Her pale eyes glowed.

Mrs. Craggs turned again to watch the pillar-like form of Madame Da Costa-O'Brien and the stocky Franz Prahler, head flung cockily back. She looked at them both with a smile of grim satisfaction.

The duet ended.

The other singers burst into a spontaneous patter of applause. They looked at each other in delight.

Jean-Artaban Pivoine walked slowly across the stage between them and the duettists.

"What a pity," he said.

Madame Da Costa-O'Brien looked round sharply.

Jean-Artaban went down to the footlights and leant forward, peering into the orchestra pit.

"You played excellently, my boy," he said. "You were quite right to hold the top C there. What happened was not at all your fault, for once."

Madame Da Costa-O'Brien swept towards him.

"You referred to a top C," she said. "May I ask whether it was the top C I sang just now?"

Jean-Artaban shrugged lightly.

"It happens to all of us," he said. "I do not think it is a question of age, necessarily. I have known it happen to quite young singers if the voice has not been sufficiently prepared."

" And what do you suggest ' happened '? " asked Madame Da Costa-O'Brien.

Her voice was ice-coated.

Jean-Artaban smiled.

" Oh, it is hardly worth mentioning."

" I wish it to be mentioned."

" Really? "

Jean-Artaban looked surprised, disappointed, regretful.

" Well, then," he said, " let us not avoid the truth. My dear colleague, you were unable to hold the top C. You slid away from it. I assure you it is a matter of no great consequence. It is quite likely not to happen in performance."

Madame Da Costa-O'Brien drew herself up.

" It is a matter of considerable consequence," she said. " Because it happens not to be true. I have never slid from a top C in my life. I have my conscience as an artist. On the rare occasions when I have found my voice affected after I have begun a performance I have omitted notes I was not able to hit and hold accurately. I would scorn to do anything else."

Jean-Artaban bowed.

" Of course, madame," he said, " one has read of your remarkable integrity as an artist. It is a well-known thing."

Madame Da Costa-O'Brien nearly made the mistake of inclining her stately head in acknowledgment. But something in Jean-Artaban's tone warned her.

Just in time.

Turning away, Jean-Artaban added a remark in a voice which only just reached the ears of his listeners.

" A pity," he said, " that report has lied."

" Sir."

Only Jean-Artaban could have ignored it.

But Madame Da Costa-O'Brien was metal worthy of him. She marched forward in his wake and laid a majestic hand on his shoulder.

Jean-Artaban turned round.

" Sir, that top C was held to perfection. I require you to apologise."

Jean-Artaban smiled.

" My dear colleague," he said, " let us not make a mountain out of this little molehill. You are not immortal. You have reached the age of errors. Let us frankly admit this and we shall then be able as fellow artists to see what can be done about circumventing it."

" There is nothing to circumvent."

The statement rang round the auditorium.

Mrs. Milhorne leant forward tensely.

Mrs. Craggs sadly shook her head.

The faint gesture must have caught Mrs. Milhorne's eye. She turned to her friend.

" I thought she was okay," she said. " But did she hold the top note, or not? "

" Of course she did," said Mrs. Craggs. " Haven't you got ears? "

Up on the stage Jean-Artaban faced Madame Da Costa-O'Brien.

" Then, *hélas*, madame, we must agree to differ," he said.

" Certainly not. You can scarcely think I shall consent to sing with—with a person who can wickedly state a falsehood about my voice," Madame Da Costa-O'Brien replied.

Suddenly Don Francisco, his hands held above his head like a terrified non-combatant drawing attention to his status, ran between them.

"Jean-Artaban, Jean-Artaban," he said, "you must know you are wrong. So many people heard the top C. It was held, held perfectly. Was it not?"

He turned in wild appeal to the others.

But before they had time to answer Jean-Artaban leant down over the little Spaniard.

"Listen to me," he stormed, "I have stated that the top C was not held. Are you doubting my ear?"

"But no. Well, but yes."

"Are you doubting my ear?"

"My dear friends," Madame Da Costa-O'Brien interrupted, "it is of no consequence. I am not singing with this person. Let that be understood."

Don Francisco's head drooped.

"In that case, Jean-Artaban," he said, "I have no alternatings. The opera is impossible without Madame. Here is the only voice in the world that could sing the music. The opera is being revivalled for the first time since Prokovinski's day especially for her. I am sorry, but you must go."

Jean-Artaban smiled.

The cat with the whisky-laced cream.

"If I go," he said, "I sue. If I sue, you go."

"But—but——"

The little Spaniard looked from side to side as if he hoped that somewhere he would spy a loophole in the very laws of truth. But to no avail.

He turned to Madame Da Costa-O'Brien.

"Madame, you see my position. If Jean-Artaban goes,

my whole plans for the Flinwich Festival tumble in ruinations. But if you will not consenting to sing, no *Death of A Fat God* can there be."

Madame Da Costa-O'Brien shook her head from side to side. It was as if a stone deity had moved in dreadful negative.

" There are things that are not possible," she said. " We cannot appear on the same stage with this person. There is no more to be said."

She turned.

Slowly, inevitably, majestically she progressed towards the door of the Pasha Selim's house.

Some of the chorus who were near her path stepped precipitately back.

Madame Da Costa-O'Brien crossed Pasha Selim's threshold. There was a scurry of feet as the onlookers hurried to the other side of the set. Madame Da Costa-O'Brien proceeded at the same unhurrying pace. She entered the corridor that led to the stage door. One or two hardy spirits followed her at a distance. She reached the stage door. From the row of pegs there she took, in a gesture of stone-like dignity, a massive black cloak.

Its heavy folds hung for a moment motionless in the air as she flung it across her wide shoulders. Then the voluminous garment fell in seemly lines about her broad form.

The stage doorkeeper opened the door and held it wide. Madame Da Costa-O'Brien sailed through.

There was a huge Rolls-Royce waiting in the dingy street. Madame Da Costa-O'Brien entered it. After a moment's pause it slowly gathered way. A knot of onlookers watched huddled together by the stage door. The great car glided to the end of the short street. It turned the corner. It vanished from sight never to be seen again in the prosaic industrial town of Flinwich.

At the stage door Don Francisco de Zayas y Tamago was white as pure marble. In a scarcely audible, choked voice he uttered a few broken words.

"He ruin my most great success. He ruin my most great chance of make for one time the critics acknowledging me. Nothing is too bad for him."

Mrs. Milhorne, who, pursued by Mrs. Craggs, had hurried out through the foyer and round to the stage door, turned to her friend.

"Who's he mean?" she asked.

Mrs. Craggs looked at the broken little Spaniard.

"I'm afraid he means Jean-Artaban," she said.

CHAPTER V

By the time Madame Da Costa-O'Brien's car had vanished almost everybody in the theatre had collected in the street outside. A little way apart from them stood Don Francisco, silent and unmoving after his single outburst. A yard or two farther down the street Mrs. Milhorne, still clutching a broom, looked at Mrs. Craggs in apprehension.

Then the tubby figure of Franz Prahler detached itself from the crowd of singers and approached Don Francisco.

"Hoop, hoop, hoop, hoop," he said. "What an exit. What an exit, *liebling*. Now we are really in the soup."

He chuckled.

A faintly cloudy look came over his bright blue eyes.

He sighed.

"But how marvellous we were singing together, Madame Da Costa-O'Brien and I," he said. "Wasn't it stupendous? You know, she thought I couldn't do it. So early in the morning, without any warming up. But I did, eh? Wasn't I good? Really good?"

He peered inquiringly into Don Francisco's utterly woebegone face.

When after some little while he had still got no answer he tapped the dumbfounded Spaniard sharply on the shoulder.

"Hey, *liebling*," he said, "wasn't I good in the duet? I bet she had been practising already to-day, the old cow. But what a voice, all the same. No one else could have sung it with me so well."

Don Francisco looked up.

"Yes," he said, "that so. No one else. No one else in the widey world. And the Presses, they don't take a damn of notice about the Flinwich Festival any more. You saw how much they are giving us for the other first nights? Five lines, ten."

His face convulsed with rage.

"*Ja*, that is bad," Franz Prahler agreed. "But you don't have anybody much singing for you, no? You have old Jean-Artaban, and he is a bit someone and Clarissa Glass she is so beautiful and sexy. But the rest, until I come for *Seraglio* to-night, pfui."

Don Francisco went on looking at the grimy pavement.

"But you wait," Franz said. "For me they come, the critics."

"But you cannot be singing in *Death of A Fat God* by yourself," Don Francisco said gloomily.

For a moment the tubby little tenor contemplated this possibility.

"No," he said at last, "for the duets there must be someone good, to sing with me. A voice of silver for my voice of gold, no?"

Don Francisco could not bring himself to answer directly.

"They would have all coming to *Death of A Fat God*," he muttered. "They would have seen. At last they would have acknowledge me. And then at the Met I would not be a laughing stocks. At L'Opéra they would not be nodding the heads."

Franz Prahler clapped his hands together suddenly.

The little pop made the wiry Spaniard at his side jump as if a charge of electricity had been put under him.

"But of course," Franz said, "but this is wonderful."

He turned enthusiastically to Don Francisco.

"Didn't I tell you that everything always works well for me?" he said.

Don Francisco glared at him.

Franz took him by both shoulders.

"Didn't I tell you just now," he said, "for me everything always goes well?"

"No."

"No? Well, it does, *liebling*, it does. Take this morning. Madame Da Costa-O'Brien sings like an angel and then, poof, away she goes. Bad, yes?"

"Ruinings."

"But, look, here all the time I have my pupil, the so wonderful Australian little girl, Mary Arthur. All the time I tell her 'No, you cannot make your début yet.'

When it comes, I tell her, she must in a flash make the name of Franz Prahler ring round the world for a new reason. And all the time she is learning. I am making her. I am driving her. And now to-day is the time come. She will sing the Goose Girl."

Don Francisco shook his head.

" My friend," he said, " you know *Death of A Fat God*. Only once in the history of the world has it been possible to sing. For the great Xaria Glistanova, Prokovinski he wrote it. And twenty years ago Madame Da Costa-O'Brien she was going to sing it at Dallas, Texas, only something happen. So all this time, nothings, no ones, silence."

" But, yes, I know *Death of A Fat God*," Franz shouted. " Of course I know it. I have been practising the role of the Shepherd for weeks. And who have I been practising my duets with? With little Mary Arthur of course, with my first and only pupil, the little girl I heard singing so out of tune in the hotel where she cleaned the rooms in Sydney. She will sing the Goose Girl. She will make my name all over again."

" I tell you it is the most impossible."

Don Francisco was shouting now, too.

Franz puffed himself out again.

" Listen, *liebling*," he said, " do you think I would consent to sing the Shepherd in public if the Goose Girl could not manage the part? Do you think I'm a fool, *liebling*? "

This argument seemed to impress Don Francisco. Slowly he looked at Franz. Slowly a pallid ray of hope came into his desolated face.

" Yes," said Franz, " yes, to-morrow we have a new

rehearsal. You shall hear her. And if she doesn't pass, if you don't like her, then we forget all about the opera, huh? Perhaps instead I sing a special performance of *The Merry Widow*. You like, yes? "

Don Francisco looked up, pale but resolute.

" I hear her to-morrow," he said.

::   ::

Mrs. Craggs and Mrs. Milhorne were not the only onlookers the next day when the rehearsal with the unknown Mary Arthur took place. All of the stage staff who did not have other jobs in the daytime were there as well as the entire corps of artists whether they had parts in *Death of A Fat God* or not.

Mrs. Milhorne surveyed the theatre. It had an air of excited bustle in spite of the pallid daylight creeping in and the cold chandelier hanging dead above them.

" Almost like the real thing, isn't it, dear? " she said to Mrs. Craggs. " Fancy having the orchestra and all. Is that to make sure she can sing loud enough? "

" They got to rehearse same as the others," said Mrs. Craggs. " Just like we got our work to do. I don't know as how we ought to have left the circle bar anyhow."

" But I couldn't have been stuck away in there with this little Mary Arthur having her try-out down here, I couldn't really. I feel for that girl, I do. I know what it's like having to face everybody like that."

" Oh, do you, dear? " said Mrs. Craggs.

" Well—Well, there was that time I went up to give evidence in the police court."

" I thought you wouldn't tell them you knew anything about it and didn't go after all."

" Perhaps I didn't, but I knew what it would have

been like, didn't I? Otherwise I wouldn't have refused to go, would I? Stands to reason."

Mrs. Milhorne gave a toss of her lank head.

But she could not afford to alienate Mrs. Craggs further than this. She needed accurate information too badly.

" Here," she said a moment later, " who's that there that Don Francisco's making up to in that way? "

" Don't you even know that? " said Mrs. Craggs.

" Well, it's my first time here."

Mrs. Craggs relented.

" It's Signor Boscani, the conductor. He's come specially for the new opera," she said.

" Yes," said Mrs. Milhorne approvingly, " I've heard of him."

Mrs. Craggs contented herself with a look. Which was altogether ineffective as Mrs. Milhorne was craning wildly to watch Boscani as he made his way with Don Francisco to the conductor's rostrum and had a last intensive colloquy with him there.

When it was finished Don Francisco called up to the empty stage, set now as the interior of the Church of Sant' Andrea della Valle for the next performance of *Tosca*.

" We are beginning with the little duet of Act I, the Goose Girl and the Harpy," he shouted. " No. 3."

Again Mrs. Milhorne applied for information.

" What No. 3? " she said. " Doesn't sound very romantic to me."

" It's just the way they have of finding the place," Mrs. Craggs said wearily. " It means the third separate piece in the opera."

" Oh, a number, like in *The Desert Song*."

" That's right."

" Well, what's this one going to be about? What was that about a harp? Is it going to have harp music in it? I'd like that. I like a bit of harp. Makes me go all kind of shivery down me back."

" It's not a harp : it's a harpy. That means a kind of nagger, old-fashioned like. It's the part Margherita Clarone came down to sing."

" Oh."

Mrs. Milhorne digested the information so far received.

" Well," she said, " I'm not sure that I'd like to sing a part if they can't find no better name for it than that. Harpy, indeed."

" It's a good part from all I hear," said Mrs. Craggs. " Should suit la Clarone. She got a bit of fire in her voice even if it isn't exactly always very sweet to listen to. Heard her do Azucena in *Trovatore* on the radio once, though, of course she's more of a contralto than a mezzo."

" I dare say," said Mrs. Milhorne.

Sagely.

" They must have chosen this duet to make it easy for Mary Arthur," Mrs. Craggs went on. " From what that Paul Pivoine was telling me it begins quite easy like with a little passage for the Goose Girl, but then almost at once the Harpy comes on and starts sort of going for her, and in the end she has to be able to sing well out on top of the contralto line. That'll be quite a test. Especially if la Clarone's in good voice. She's got a lot of power there, bit too much really, I suppose. But you know what these Italians are."

" I shouldn't be surprised if I got a bit of Italian blood in me somewhere," Mrs. Milhorne confessed. " I get such queer feelings come over me every now and again—— "

E

" Sssh."

Boscani had given three little impatient taps with his baton on the top of his music stand.

The orchestra began to play the prelude to the scene between the Goose Girl and the Harpy.

Mary Arthur came tripping incongruously out of the iron gates of the Attavanti Chapel. She danced around in the space intended to be the main body of the Church of Sant' Andrea and made as if she was picking the occasional flower in the meadows where she should have been tending her geese.

She was obviously very nervous and kept darting apprehensive glances at Boscani, bent over the music desk coaxing with expressive hands the exact sounds he wanted from the motley collection of orchestral players in everyday clothes. The music was not easy and Mrs. Craggs pursed her lips together and looked more intently at the slight figure of the unknown Australian girl.

" Got the figure for it more she has," whispered Mrs. Milhorne.

Mrs. Craggs made no reply.

Mary Arthur picked another imaginary flower. At the side of the stage Margherita Clarone crept darkly into sight and watched the waif-like figure of the Goose Girl with urgent jealousy. The prelude quietened and Mary Arthur straightened up. As the introductory bars to her first words were played she looked up to the sky and a slight smile came over her face.

And then pearling evenly over the murmur of the orchestra came the first delicate, cruelly high phrase. And each note was crystally in place, carrying easily out into the half-darkness of the big, empty theatre, true, liquid and filled with delight.

There was a sudden clatter in the orchestra pit. Boscani had dropped his baton in astonishment.

With an urgent wave of his long fingers he signed to the players to go on. With scarcely a falter they obeyed.

Mary Arthur's voice floated out above their accompaniment like a string of fine jewels on some dark velvet underbed. She finished her tiny song. The orchestral colouring took on a sudden deeper hue for the first bitter comment from the waiting Harpy.

And it did not come.

All eyes turned to the waiting Margherita. To find her waiting still, lost in delight at the Australian soprano's singing.

CHAPTER VI

" Yes," said Mrs. Milhorne, " I could have told you the moment I heard her voice at that first rehearsal. She's the greatest singing discovery since Caruso. Just listen to her."

Mrs. Craggs listened. Her sombre eyes lit up with pleasure.

" It's funny," she said. " Up to a few days ago no one had heard of her, and now they're talking about her in the papers and everything even before she's sung a note of her début."

Mrs. Milhorne looked at her sharply.

" Are you saying she isn't worth it? Because let me tell

you that girl's got a voice in a million if ever I heard one."

"No," said Mrs. Craggs, "I'm not saying she won't be worth it when the public's heard her. But how anyone can really say she's worth it before I don't know."

"It said so in the paper this very morning."

Mrs. Milhorne was crushing.

"Yes," said Mrs. Craggs, "they're the worst, those reporters. Look at the way they're trying to get into rehearsals and everything. It isn't proper."

"Still," said Mrs. Milhorne triumphantly, "we've kept 'em out, haven't we?"

"We have," said Mrs. Craggs.

She looked down at her broomhandle fondly.

"And just think what the first night's going to be like," Mrs. Milhorne went on. "Every seat in the house taken, some of them twice over I shouldn't wonder."

Mrs. Craggs gave a short, sharp laugh.

"Old Don Francisco'll have his heart's desire after all," she said. "Though they won't have a line to spare for all his production tricks, not if she manages it all right. I hear he's going to let loose a lot of real peacocks in the last act."

"If she manages it all right?" said Mrs. Milhorne. "There's no if about it. 'Course she'll manage. She's got the voice of a nightingale, hasn't she?"

"She's got a voice all right," Mrs. Craggs said. "But we've never seen her with an audience, have we, not a proper one? And sometimes I wonder. . . ."

Mrs. Milhorne tossed her head.

"I don't know how you can bring yourself to speak such nonsense," she said. "I tell you that voice'll be heard from one end of the world to the other before many months are out. Just listen to her now, just listen to her."

Mrs. Craggs listened again.

Mary Arthur was singing the final scene of *Death of A Fat God* to Paul Pivoine's piano accompaniment, a long soaring duet with Franz Prahler just before the coming of the Fat God himself. And certainly there was nothing in her voice to give grounds for any doubts. In all its range it had shown itself to be the astonishingly beautiful thing that had caused such a sensation in the first few phrases heard at the first rehearsal.

The duet reached its climax. Paul Pivoine abandoned for once his customary drooping attitude over the piano keyboard and leant back to deliver with the whole weight of his broad shoulders the crashing series of chords which introduced his father on the stage above. Then he launched into the accompaniment of the Fat God's opening aria.

And from the stage no voice.

Don Francisco, sitting in the first row of the stalls, leapt to his feet.

"Jean-Artaban, Jean-Artaban," he called. "It is your cueing."

There was a pause and then Jean-Artaban walked on to the stage through a pair of double doors in the Palace of the Duke of Mantua, where later that evening he would sing Rigoletto.

As soon as he appeared Don Francisco burst into a stream of indignant reproaches, too furious to be comprehensible.

Jean-Artaban stood by the footlights looking down at him. He let him go on and on with wild shouts of " Unpunctualishness " and " Unartisticated " until at last he stopped for air. But even then the towering French bass-baritone remained impassive.

" Is it all over? " he asked at last.

Don Francisco drew himself up, a little wearily.

" I have said all I want to say. Just rememberings."

" And now," said Jean-Artaban, " may I draw your attention to the score? "

" The score, the score."

Don Francisco picked up his broad copy of the score and waved it indignantly.

" You draw my attentions to the score," he said. " What happen if I draw your attentions to it? You are not making the entrance when says so the score. You are the one dropping in artisticalness."

" Please," Jean-Artaban said, " not again. I think you should not be allowed more than one outburst a day, my friend. The nerves of the rest of us must be considered."

Don Francisco almost crouched with tenseness as he flung back his reply.

" Then do what is saying the score. When comings in, in come."

" Certainly."

Jean-Artaban was momentarily calm.

" Certainly," he repeated. " I will enter when the score directs. And in the manner in which the score directs."

Don Francisco was too easy game.

" Then why you no come in now? " he burst out.

Jean-Artaban smiled.

" Because the score says ' The Fat God descends in a machine '," he replied. " And there is no machine."

Don Francisco actually tore at his curly black hair.

" But do you not understanding? " he stormed. " This is rehearse in *Rigoletto* set. If we was rehearse in *Fat God* set then in machine down you enter."

Again Jean-Artaban smiled.

" If we were rehearsing in the *Fat God* set," he said. " And, my dear friend, there is less than a week till the first performance. Is it not about time we saw this so ingenious set that we have all got to act in? "

Don Francisco closed his eyes.

" It will be there, it will be there," he said.

" Ah, yes, no doubt it will be there, and the doors will be too narrow and there will be so wonderful heavy drapes everywhere so that the voices are all smothered up and those terrible peacocks will make their messes everywhere and peck the chorus. That sort of thing we are used to. That we can insist on having changed."

Don Francisco shut his heavy score with a bang.

" If we are going to be listen to this," he said, " no more rehearse we will have."

" Yes," answered Jean-Artaban, " you are right, my friend. There is no need to go on with rehearsal."

He shrugged.

" After all," he said, " if the finale is going to turn out to be impossible to stage, why rehearse it? "

" Impossible to stage, impossible to stage? I, Don Francisco de Zayas y Tamago, have staged it."

" You have dreamt, Don Francisco. But where are your dreams come to life? It is easy to read in a score ' the Fat God comes down in a machine ' but if you cannot design a machine for the god to come down in, what use are your dreams about it all? "

" But the machine is designed, almost."

" Almost. Almost. And in less than a week I ride in it. Have you thought what would happen if it fell from the top of the theatre on to the stage with me in it at the first night? I suppose your production would at last get the attention of the critics then? "

Don Francisco looked up to the roof of the theatre high above. From where he was standing it was possible to see up behind the proscenium arch into the high flies with the myriads of ropes disappearing into the darkness. It looked a very long way up.

" The machine will work," he said.

His mouth set in an obstinate line.

" That I prefer to believe when I see it," said Jean-Artaban. " You will excuse a word of warning between old friends, but a death on the first night of the opera with such an exclusive audience to watch it would hardly be a desirable thing."

At the back of the auditorium Mrs. Craggs pursed her lips.

" All the same, my boy," she said, " as it would be your death I bet there's one or two that wouldn't be sorry."

Mrs. Milhorne looked at her with eyes opening wider and wider. But before she had had time to say anything a further commotion up on the stage distracted her.

Jean-Artaban was leaning forward over the footlights, peering down into the orchestra pit where his son was sitting hunched up in the little pool of light coming from the bulb over the music rest of the piano.

" Well, down there," Jean-Artaban said in a voice which rang round the big, empty half-dark theatre, " are you not going to condescend to play for us to-day? Is the maestro indisposed? Should we go home and come again another day when he feels that he cares to let his fingers caress the keys of the piano? "

Paul looked up.

" I thought you were talking, Father," he said.

" Yes, yes," said Jean-Artaban. " You think your father is talking, so what do you do? You go to sleep. It doesn't matter to you, I suppose, what your father happens to say. No, he is only an old fool. While he is speaking we can go to sleep."

" I wasn't asleep."

" Now we are getting lies. You weren't asleep, were you? Then why when we are ready to sing are you not ready to play? Answer me that."

No answer.

" Answer, my boy."

Still from the black pit between the stage and the stalls no sound.

Jean-Artaban walked along the footlights to a position where he could see something of his son's sunk face.

" Now," he shouted suddenly, " now, I will have an answer. Why were you not ready to play? "

Still silence.

" Very well," Jean-Artaban said, " then if you behave like a child, I will behave like the father of a child. If you do not respond at once, I will come down and give you a good box on the head."

Paul Pivoine looked up.

" I didn't know you were ready," he muttered.

" What's that? Speak up, boy."

No reply again.

" Speak up. I will hear what you have got to say."

Now Paul looked up at his father.

" I did not know that you were ready," he shouted.

" Ah, excellent. At last we have a reply. Very well then see that another time you do know when we are ready. Since when have singers had to wait on the pleasure of a damn' rehearsal pianist? "

Abruptly Paul began to play.

He stumbled more than usually over the notes.

At the back of the theatre Mrs. Craggs held her breath and looked at Jean-Artaban. But the huge bass-baritone was apparently more pleased with the effect he had had on his son's playing than he was put out by the numerous wrong notes of his accompaniment. He sang his aria with relish, holding on to each low note for all it was worth while his son desperately lingered over the piano part to keep in time with him.

The aria merged into a furious duet with the tenor, and this too Jean-Artaban palpably enjoyed. With cunning he used his big voice to swamp the golden lyric tones of the tubby little Austrian.

But towards the end of the long duet Franz Prahler began to get irritated. Up till now he had been singing more or less half-voice, but suddenly he let himself go. His voice was nothing like as strong as Jean-Artaban's, but not for nothing had he acquired his reputation. His airy, golden notes seemed to soar above the deeper bass rumblings, and the louder and worse Jean-Artaban sang, the more sweetly and easily did Franz outdo him.

The duet ended.

At this point the Fat God should have retired dying from the field, but Jean-Artaban made no move to quit the stage.

Instead, even though Paul was still playing the short

linking passage between the duet and the Goose Girl's aria of thanks for her deliverance—the famous, almost impossible coloratura piece which shares the opera's name—his father stayed where he was. He began talking.

"That wasn't bad, Franz," he said.

No one took any notice, except Paul who played a little bit more loudly.

"No," Jean-Artaban said in a voice which could not be ignored, "that was not bad at all."

"Sssh, ssh," said Don Francisco from his seat in the front row of the stalls.

Jean-Artaban showed no signs of having heard.

"You know," he said, "there were times when I thought my voice was not really dominating yours."

Franz looked rather as if he had been suddenly puffed up by a shot of compressed air. But Jean-Artaban seemed not to be aware of the effect he was having.

"Of course," he went on, "when it comes to the performance I realise I shall have to be careful to sing it down and let it seem that your voice is the stronger."

He laughed.

"It would never do for the hero not to vanquish the evil Fat God," he said. "At least not on the first night. For Scarpia to rise again at a routine performance of *Tosca*, especially when the soprano was so bad, well, that is a little treat for the audience once in a while. But I have my artistic conscience."

He walked over to where the tubby little Austrian was standing and patted him on the back.

"No," he said, "you needn't worry. On the first night you will appear to have the great voice. Jean-Artaban will abnegate himself in the interests of art once again."

" But please not to bother," said Franz.

" No, no. I must. I know you would not wish it. But we have to think of the critics. In the end the Fat God must appear to lose. Very well then, he shall lose. After all, you and I and all the real connoisseurs of voices know the truth."

Franz puffed out his chest.

" Yes," he said, " I know the truth. You have the voice of a bull, Jean-Artaban, but you do not know how to use it. Any day I can place mine on top of yours. Don't you worry about that, *liebling*."

Jean-Artaban smiled pityingly and turned to little Mary Arthur.

" Well, my girl," he said, " I hope someone has warned you about tenors before you embark on a great career in the world of opera."

Mary Arthur looked at him but did not answer. She held her body rigid from embarrassment.

Jean-Artaban shrugged.

" Of course," he said, " with the teacher you had, one could not expect you to know the whole truth. But, happily, you will meet men of understanding, who are not tenors, and they will be able to enlighten you."

He crossed the stage to where the little Australian girl was standing and attempted to chuck her under the chin.

" Here," she said in a cutting Australian accent, " you take your filthy hands off me."

Jean-Artaban was not disconcerted. He held his two great hands wide in a gesture of delight.

" Ah," he said, " what innocence. What delightfully simple notions. I see that indeed Franz has taught you nothing."

He shook his head sadly.

" Never mind, my dear," he said, " one day you will grow up and learn. It may be a hard lesson, but one day you will find out that all men who offer you a friendly word of advice are not wicked wolves prowling all about you. Will you remember old Jean-Artaban then? "

He bent inquiringly close to Mary.

She looked up at him but said nothing.

" Ah," said Jean-Artaban, " Franz, you old devil, you have a lot to answer for. You have put the spell of Wotan on your little Brunnhilde. Now she sleeps. But who knows in what form her awakening Siegfried will come? "

He looked down with complacency at the vast stretch of his chest and stomach.

Mary Arthur turned and walked over to the low ledge-seat where later Rigoletto, the deformed jester, would cower under the curse of the ancient Count Monterone. She sat down and appeared to be unconcernedly examining her nails.

Jean-Artaban gave her a single glance and then returned to Franz.

" Well," he said, " the poor girl may be unlucky in some ways, but she is lucky in others."

He checked himself and allowed the enigmatic remark to hang in the air.

Foolishly Franz took it up.

" You mean to have a so lovely voice, *liebling*? " he said.

The effort to bring the conversation into normal friendliness was all too plain.

Jean-Artaban looked surprised.

" Why no," he said, " that was not exactly what I meant, as a matter of fact."

" Oh, then what did you mean? You are very mysterious this morning, *liebling*."

Jean-Artaban smiled.

" Do you really want to know what I meant? " he
asked.

Franz looked suddenly deflated and uncomfortable.
But he put a good face on it.

" Why, of course, *liebling*," he said. " One is always
delighted and interested in what you say."

" Then I'll tell you."

The note of unpleasantness in the French singer's voice
was plain and purposeful.

" I'll tell you. I think the little creature is lucky
because she has the sort of voice which no amount of so-
called teaching can ruin. It is a great natural voice. If it
had been a poor one, she would have been ear-splitting to
hear by now."

Franz's chubby pink face was white.

" You. You."

He could find no words.

His whole tubby form shook with violent rage and he
took a step forward as if he was on the point of hurling
himself at the huge, flabby-looking Frenchman.

But Jean-Artaban simply looked at him.

" You seem put out by hearing the truth," he said.
" However I am not discomposed by that. I have spoken
the truth to so many people in my life who would rather
not hear it that I am used to its effects."

" The truth."

Franz was holding himself in with difficulty. His face
had now gone from white to deeply furious purple.

" Yes," Jean-Artaban went on, " I am rather good at

knowing the truth. I know the truth about a lot of things. About the origins of a great many of my colleagues so-called, for instance, where they were born and how long ago, all that sort of thing."

His fairly innocuous words seemed to have a startling effect on the enraged Austrian. He looked at Jean-Artaban as if he was hearing the revelations of a prophet. The purple left his face slowly and blotchily.

He turned abruptly and walked to the far edge of the stage.

" Excuse me, Don Francisco, *liebling*," he said in a curiously muted voice, " we have been interrupting the rehearsal with our talk. Please go on."

Don Francisco looked at him intently but Franz said no more. He took his stance to sing the final duet with Mary Arthur. She in her turn got up and came across towards him. Don Francisco signalled to Paul to play.

But hardly had he touched the keys of the piano when there was another interruption.

From the back of the auditorium behind Mrs. Craggs and Mrs. Milhorne came a shrill female voice.

" This is right. This must be the way. And I think you will find that they welcome me."

A moment later a very old woman, dressed from head to foot in black and leaning heavily on a silver-headed cane, came in. She was followed by a nondescript dumpy man a good few years her junior. He was respectably but rather poorly dressed and was carrying a dark tartan rug over one arm and a small plastic hold-all, which he gripped as if it was as valuable as a bank messenger's cash case.

The old lady took one look at the theatre and straightened her skeleton shoulders beneath the heavy lace shawl.

She walked jerkily but quite quickly down towards the lighted stage. Everybody looked at her.

Neither Mrs. Craggs nor Mrs. Milhorne had felt able to ask her whether she had any business in the theatre.

It was only when she got into the full light coming from the stage that anybody spoke.

Then it was Jean-Artaban.

He looked at her closely, with an air of utter incredulity.

" But it cannot be. It is altogether impossible," he said.

CHAPTER VII

THE OLD LADY in her rustling black silks looked up at Jean-Artaban. She leant on her silver-headed cane and smiled very slightly.

" I do not know who you are, young man," she said, " but I assure you it is as you think."

She straightened her back and abandoned the support of the stick.

" Yes," she said, " it is I, the person who was once known to the world as Xaria Glistanova."

Her announcement could not have had greater effect. Nobody spoke, but Don Francisco stood as if he had suddenly been transformed into a lifelike statue and Franz's mouth dropped open and stayed wide.

In the whole theatre only Mrs. Milhorne remained unaffected.

" Yes," she said to Mrs. Craggs in a loud whisper, " but who's whoever she said she was? "

Mrs. Craggs slowly turned.

" Xaria Glistanova," she said. " Xaria Glistanova was one of the great sopranos of all time. She followed Patti and Melba, and there's some as says she was better than either of them."

She looked down the sloping length of the deserted auditorium at the aged, bony figure in black standing erectly by the rail of the orchestra pit.

" Good heavens," she said, " she must be ninety now if she's a day. Everybody thought she was dead."

And up on the stage everybody still looked as if they were in the presence of a ghost. It was Jean-Artaban who was first to come out of the spell. He did so with characteristic bravura.

" La Glistanova," he shouted.

And taking two great strides to the footlights he bounded down into a small clear space among the litter of chairs and music stands in the orchestra pit. Then as quickly he grasped the rail of the pit and with a heave that made the heavy barrier groan and tremble he vaulted over into the space in front of the first row of the stalls where Xaria Glistanova proudly stood.

" La Glistanova," he repeated.

And he dropped on one knee in homage.

His huge head, topped with the crown of short blond hair, came up almost to Xaria Glistanova's face as he took the hand that was not holding the silver-headed stick and carried it to his lips.

" I, Jean-Artaban Pivoine, the greatest bass-baritone voice of the world to-day, do homage," he boomed.

Xaria Glistanova took her hand easily from his grasp and rested it with the other on the plain silver knob of her cane.

F

She closed her eyes for an instant.

" I'm afraid I don't know your work," she said in a voice which though quiet carried clearly to every part of the darkened auditorium. " I don't hear any opera these days. I haven't done for quite a number of years."

Jean-Artaban rose to his feet. The disappointment was clearly expressed on his face though he succeeded in saying nothing.

Xaria Glistanova slowly raised her head and looked round at the singers on the stage.

" Indeed," she said, " it was only by chance that I heard that *Death of A Fat God* was to be revived. I am sorry to say that it was the first I had heard of the Flinwich Festival. However. . . ."

She substituted a slight weary gesture for the end of the sentence, and then turned to the little, rather crouching man who was her companion.

She smiled at him.

" It was only at my husband's insistence that I decided to come down here," she said, " and to offer you my memories of what Prokovinski had to say about the work when we first produced it."

Don Francisco shook himself slightly.

" Madame Glistanova," he said.

He could hardly express himself for wonder.

" Madame Glistanova, that you should be alive, that you should be here."

He shook his head incredulously.

" I had no ideas," he said.

He came forward and bowed low with sharply clicking heels.

" May I present myself? " he said. " Don Francisco

de Zayas y Tamago, grandee of Spain, and Director of the Flinwich Festival."

He bowed again.

Xaria Glistanova inclined her head a little and looked at him steadily under her creased and lined lids.

"And may I in all humblenesses accept your kindly offers. To know the very mind of Prokovinski, it is the most joy for a producer."

A slight smile moved the corners of Xaria Glistanova's mouth.

"That is as may be," she said. "After all, the mind of Prokovinski may prove to be different from the mind of the producer, and what shall we do then?"

Don Francisco squared his slight shoulders.

"Then we shall be proudly to cede to him who would cede to no other body," he said.

Xaria Glistanova raised her eyebrows fractionally.

"Well," she said, "times change and perhaps what poor Prokovinski thought good all those many years ago would not please the public to-day."

"We shall not please the public : we shall please the spirit of Prokovinski the great."

Xaria Glistanova turned and looked at the dusky rows of plush seats climbing away from her into almost complete obscurity under the faint reflections of the great unlit chandelier.

"But the public will hear the opera," she said.

Her husband came forward until he was standing beside her. He moved with a curious, sideways-looking, obsequious step and seemed to be seeking attention only against his own desire.

He bowed to Don Francisco.

" I wonder," he said in a lisping, very quiet voice, " if I might be so bold as to ask if I could lay Madame Glistanova's rug in one of the seats here in the front row."

He glanced almost furtively at the plush tip-up chairs.

" She has to conserve her energies," he said. "And she will not do it of her own accord."

A fleeting half-smile.

" It is my privilege to insist that she looks after herself."

Don Francisco was instantly all contrition.

" But, of course, Mr.—er Monsieur—er—— "

" My name is actually Einfalt, Heinrich Einfalt."

Xaria Glistanova's little husband waved the matter aside.

" But, of course, Mr. Einfalt, do everything that is necessary. Ask for whatever you wants."

Don Francisco with widespread arms put the total resources of the late Simon Creassels at Xaria Glistanova's service.

" Thank you, thank you," Heinrich Einfalt said.

He took the dark blue-green tartan rug from under his arm and spread it diligently out over one of the seats not far from where Don Francisco had been sitting directing the rehearsal. Then from the little plastic zip-bag he took a number of objects and arranged them solicitously on the seat next to the one on which he had placed the rug. There was a leather-bound score of *Death of A Fat God*, two medicine bottles and a small graduated glass, an extra shawl and a spectacles case.

When they were all disposed to his satisfaction he took a quick look at Don Francisco from under one arm as he bent over his improvised table.

"It is my privilege," he said. "Three kings offered their hands in marriage to the great singer, Xaria Glistanova. She is now my wife."

He straightened up and went over to the slightly stooping figure leaning patiently on the silver-knobbed cane.

"Come, my dear," he said. "All is ready."

She smiled at him.

"My poor, good Heinrich," she said. "You take so much trouble."

Heinrich Einfalt did not reply in words. The look of dog devotion he gave his wife as he led her to the rug-spread seat was an eloquent response.

He settled her slowly into her place.

It was evident from the painful deliberation of her movements that, although she remained completely impassive, she did in fact suffer a good deal from the infirmities of great age. Her husband, once she looked comfortable, crouched in the seat on the far side of the little array of medicaments and necessities.

"Don Francisco," said Xaria Glistanova in the voice which carried so effectively, "please continue. I shall watch if I may and should any suggestions occur to me I will not fail to pass them on to you at a time to suit your convenience."

"But no," Don Francisco said, " on the other hand you must at all cost interrupt whenever you wishes."

Xaria Glistanova did not renew her protestations. She smiled slightly and inclined her head.

For an instant or two Don Francisco watched her as if he expected to hear from her lips the actual voice of the dead Russian composer decreeing his next actions. But when she sat in immobile silence he turned at last to his score and consulted it flurriedly.

"We go on from page 324," he announced. "Jean-Artaban."

Jean-Artaban slowly opened his score and found the place. He looked at it for a little while and seeming to find no objections to the passage Don Francisco had indicated slowly went back up on to the stage, this time through the pass door instead of over the orchestra pit.

When he had positioned himself amid the receding vistas of the Duke of Mantua's court Don Francisco called over to Paul Pivoine to start playing.

The bizarre music of the great Russian composer floated out into the half-darkness of the empty theatre. Xaria Glistanova in her rug nest in the front row of the stalls grew visibly straighter.

The moment came for Jean-Artaban to sing.

And he was silent.

"Jean-Artaban," Don Francisco called.

He glanced along the row of plush seats to the silhouetted figure of Xaria Glistanova. She remained still as a statue.

Don Francisco looked apprehensively up on to the stage where the French bass-baritone was standing looking into space.

"Jean-Artaban, it is your cueing," he said tentatively.

Still Jean-Artaban remained silent.

"Jean-Artaban, your cueing."

A trace of exasperation.

And no reaction whatever from Jean-Artaban.

"Jean-Artaban, Jean-Artaban, have you gone the most deaf?"

The huge singer moved his head and looked contemptuously in Don Francisco's direction.

"When I hear my music, I sing."

"But your music has been played, Jean-Artaban."

The big blond head nodded in curt negative.

"But did you not hear?"

In the back of the theatre Emma Craggs sighed under her stern hat.

"Some people'll never learn," she said.

"What was that, dear?" said Mrs. Milhorne.

"Oh, nothing, dear. Nothing."

Don Francisco hopped out of his seat.

"Did you not hear your music?" he shouted up to Jean-Artaban.

"I heard someone playing the piano," Jean-Artaban said.

He shrugged. Massively.

"I did not recognise what was being played," he added. "But certainly it was not the music of Prokovinski."

And only now did he glance at the upright figure of Xaria Glistanova.

She remained unmoving.

"Jean-Artaban," said Don Francisco with exaggerated politeness, "that was your son. He was play the music for your cueing. He was play what was wroted in the score."

Jean-Artaban shook his head.

"I say 'Yes'," Don Francisco shouted.

A little jet of pure fury.

"I think not," replied Jean-Artaban.

Each word spaced at a distance from the other. Maddeningly.

He took a step nearer the footlights and leant forward in the direction of Xaria Glistanova.

"Fortunately," he said, "we have an impeccable judge. Madame, am I not right? That music we have just heard bore no relation to the intentions of the great Prokovinski, did it?"

Everybody looked frankly at the old woman swathed in the tartan travelling-rug like a fragile china figure in some dark protective wrapping.

She moved her head very slightly to look across the barrier of the orchestra pit at the slumped shape of Paul Pivoine staring sullenly at the yellowed keys of the rehearsal piano.

"It was not Prokovinski," she said quietly.

A tiny shrug.

"But then the life of Prokovinski's music is in the orchestral colour, as we all know. For a piano rendering, what we have just heard was well played."

She turned in her seat and looked across at Paul with mild approval.

Paul, just before she delivered her verdict, had actually raised his head from his gloomy contemplation of the tarnished and chipped keys. Now he flushed deeply and irregularly all over his broad face.

Like the piston of some heavy engine he shot up from the piano stool and hovered for a moment in the air.

But instead of descending again as smoothly as the piston, he turned and blundered his way suddenly towards the narrow, black tunnel through which the musicians made their entrance to the pit.

He was gone before anybody properly realised what he was doing. Behind him a chair, knocked sideways against a music stand, slowly slithered to the ground. As it fell it hit into a second music stand and sent it clattering to the ground.

After the noise of its fall there was a short silence.

Jean-Artaban, who from the stage above had not been able to make out clearly what had happened, walked along the footlights and then peered over into the pit. It took him some little time to satisfy himself that his son had deserted his post. When he had made sure he turned and tossed off an inconsequent shrug.

" Really," he said, " one should not allow children to have any part in a serious business like opera. One has one's responsibilities to one's fellow artists after all."

He walked slowly across the mock marble magnificence of the Duke of Mantua's court and stood leaning against an ornate Corinthian column at the back of the stage.

The column swayed slightly under his weight.

In the front row of the stalls Don Francisco buried his head in his hands.

" No, no," he groaned, " not to-day. Yesterday, yes. But to-day I cannot playing the piano for the rehearse. To-day is too important to give the directings. And with such a chances too."

He lifted his head from his hands to stare tragically at the unmoving Xaria Glistanova.

Suddenly her husband, crouching in his seat and watching the erect form of his wife as intently as a fielder watching the nearby batsman, rose to his feet.

" Please," he said, " if I can perhaps be of any help. I play the piano. Not well, but I have accompanied my wife when she sang. It is enough."

Don Francisco leapt up. He rushed along the row of seats and seized Heinrich Einfalt by both hands.

" My dear sir," he said, " my most dear sir, you have save us. Please to play."

He turned and shot a quick bow at Madame Glistanova, who smiled calmly.

" Henrich," she said, " by all means play. But remember to play with force. You have got to make music for everyone here."

Her little husband nodded his head up and down like a wild puppet.

" Yes, yes, Xaria," he lisped. " Yes, yes, I will do it. Yes, I remember. You have pointed it out before. I lack force. Yes, force. That is what I want : I will remember it."

" Then you must be coming this ways," Don Francisco said. " You go through here, the pass door, and turn to—— "

He paused for an intense moment to translate to himself.

" Yes, turn to the rightly. And then you see the pit."

Heinrich Einfalt smiled nervously, darted in the direction of the pass door, changed his mind, turned and smiled tentatively round again and at last vanished.

Jean-Artaban came striding quickly down to the front of the stage. He bowed to Xaria Glistanova.

" Madame," he said, " we are all greatly indebted to you. I cannot sufficiently apologise."

He inclined his head.

" My son has once more disgraced the family name," he added.

Heinrich Einfalt emerged hesitantly into the orchestra pit and sidled across towards the piano.

" Well," said Mrs. Milhorne, at the back of the auditorium, " perhaps we shall be able to get on a bit now."

" Oh, yes," said Mrs. Craggs, " we'll be able to get on a bit for the present. But, mark my words, he'll find something else to do before long."

" Who do you mean, dear? " Mrs. Milhorne asked. " Not that soppy little creature what says he's married to Madame Glista-whatsit? "

" No, not him," Mrs. Craggs said. " He'll never make a fuss of that sort. No, it's Jean-Artaban, I mean."

" Oh, yes? "

Mrs. Craggs shook her head.

" He's the sort that goes on and on till somebody loses all control and does something terrible," she said.

Mrs. Milhorne looked down the slanting rows of plush seats at the brightly lit stage. Jean-Artaban was just beginning to sing. He was in good voice. The cruel music seemed to spur him on.

" No," Mrs. Milhorne said, " I don't believe anyone with a lovely voice like that's got real evil in him. I can't think that."

Mrs. Craggs was also looking at the towering blond-headed French singer.

" Voice has got nothing to do with it," she snapped. " There'll be trouble before long because of him. And so there would be if he was Chaliapin himself."

CHAPTER VIII

WITH VIGOROUSLY deft brush strokes Mrs. Craggs was sweeping Franz Prahler's dressing-room. Mrs. Milhorne appeared in the open doorway. She leant her own broom against the iron rail of the gallery off which the row of " gentlemen's side " dressing-rooms ran.

For a few moments she watched Mrs. Craggs in silence. The pile of dust and rubbish in the centre of the floor grew.

" You know," said Mrs. Milhorne, " if you'd have told me a fortnight ago that I'd have wanted to watch the same opera more than once I'd have said you was barmy."

" I did tell you."

" Yes, I wouldn't have believed it. It's funny how you don't know about a thing for years and when you come across it like, all of a sudden it's as if it was part of your life and always had been. Comes of having a soul, I suppose."

Mrs. Craggs neatly flicked a wilted carnation on top of the dust pile.

" 'Course," Mrs. Milhorne said, " it wasn't as if it was the same opera quite, was it? "

" Well, we didn't get Baron Scarpia resurrecting himself to-night," Mrs. Craggs said.

She spoke grimly.

" Yes, that's what I meant. And this is the way it's meant to be, is it? "

" It is."

" They don't never do it the other way round? "

" I never heard of it. And from what they was saying after the last time I don't think anyone was ever so puffed up with their own conceit as to have done it before. They thought it was real terrible."

" Did they? Well, it's funny but it seemed to give it more of a thrill to me like."

Mrs. Milhorne leant against the door jamb and pondered.

" Yes," she said, " I think in many ways it was better the way he did it the first time. I really do. But then, of course, I'm always one for the unconventional as you might say."

She simpered.

Mrs. Craggs knelt down, grimaced a little as her rheumatic hip sent a sharp jab of pain up her back, and began sweeping the pile of dust and rubbish into her dust-pan.

Mrs. Milhorne shifted herself slightly to get the edge of the jamb more comfortably under her prominent shoulder blades.

" I wonder why he didn't do it our way to-night? " she said. " If I see him I'm going to ask. An artist like him must feel ever so isolated at times. I dare say he'd like to know he gets a bit of appreciation from one person at least. Yes, I think I'll hang about a bit and see if I can catch him."

" You're a fool."

" Here, what do you mean? Just because two lonely spirits call to each other, it doesn't mean you've any right to go using abuse."

" Don't you know why he didn't mess about to-night? "

" I wouldn't call it messing about. More like daring unconventionality, I'd say."

" There's some who'd call it a darn sight worse than messing about."

Mrs. Milhorne tossed her head.

" Why did he do it this way to-night then, if you're so clever? " she said.

" 'Cos Xaria Glistanova was in watching the last half. That's why. He didn't want her to go thinking he could do a thing as bad as that."

" Well, I don't think you're right, that's all. I think it was more that the wild mood didn't seize him. Anyhow, what's she want to go poking her nose in for if she isn't going to watch the whole show from the front and pay for the pleasure, too? "

" I don't suppose she much wanted to see *Tosca* for about the five hundredth time, not done by this lot, anyhow. She came for the special rehearsal, that's what."

" What special rehearsal? I never heard nothing about a special rehearsal."

" I don't suppose they're going to avail themselves of your talents to-night, dear," Mrs. Craggs said.

The rare asperity helped her to get over the unpleasant business of rising from her knees.

She groaned under her breath.

" There's no call to be sarky, I'm sure," said Mrs. Milhorne.

A toss of her lank hair.

Mrs. Craggs relented.

" I only happened to hear about it myself by chance," she said. " There's a special late rehearsal been called and they're going to put up the set for the last act of the new opera for it. It's because they're worried about this god's car business."

"Yes," said Mrs. Milhorne, "I ain't never been able to make out what all that's about neither. Though I do know Jean-Artaban's been creating about it something awful."

"Lots of nonsense if you ask me."

"Well, it may be and it may be not. An artist like Jean-Artaban's got to live on his nerves, and when you're doing that a little thing can make an 'ell of a difference. I know. I got nerves, too."

Mrs. Craggs looked round Franz Prahler's dressing-room. Everything seemed to be in its proper place.

"All the same," Mrs. Milhorne said, "what is this car they keep talking about? I thought the opera was meant to be in the real old-fashioned days."

"'Course it is. It isn't a motor car they mean. It's more a sort of chariot. The god comes down in it out of the sky."

"Oh, I see. Sounds a bit silly to me though."

"It's opera."

Mrs. Craggs, carrying her dustpan in one hand and broom in the other, pushed past Mrs. Milhorne out on to the gallery.

She surveyed the row of dressing-room doors. Most of them were still closed. She looked across at the opposite gallery. There, too, the dressing-rooms appeared to be still in use.

"Won't be no hope of getting into that Miss Glass's room till heaven knows when," she said. "The time she spends on that face of hers."

" She's a lovely person," said Mrs. Milhorne. " Really lovely."

" Pity she hasn't got a voice to go with it then," Mrs. Craggs said.

She inspected the doors once again.

" Might as well go over the other side and just see if any of them's left the door just ajar," she said.

She stumped off round the ironwork fly gallery.

Just as she arrived at the other side of the theatre she saw Xaria Glistanova, accompanied by her husband who was looking more anxious than ever, slowly ascending the staircase from the stage. Mrs. Craggs pressed back against the iron rail of the gallery to keep well out of the way.

Madame Glistanova's approach was painful. She tapped at each of the narrow ironwork steps with her black stick and then laboriously hoisted herself upward, while behind her Heinrich Einfalt darted in and supported her.

When she got to the last step but two, she caught sight of Mrs. Craggs.

" I wonder if you would be so kind as to take my arm," she said. " I think the step with the turn may be more than I can manage."

Mrs. Craggs came forward and took the aged singer's matchstick elbow. Hindered rather than helped by the efforts of Heinrich Einfalt below she succeeded in hoisting the old lady on to the gallery. She heard her breath coming in light rapid puffs in the gloom.

" Now," she said at last, " perhaps you would also be good enough to tell me which is Miss Clarissa Glass's dressing-room."

" Certainly," Mrs. Craggs said. " It's the third along.

I know she's there, but whether she's finished getting herself ready or not I couldn't say."

" Oh, it's of no consequence that she should be dressed," Xaria Glisanova said. " I wished only to offer her a word of congratulation on her performance."

She inclined her head towards Mrs. Craggs and set off for Clarissa's dressing-room with her little bent-framed husband fussing along behind.

Mrs. Craggs stood for a moment watching them.

Heinrich Einfalt sidled round in front of his wife and tapped on the dressing-room door.

" Who the hell is it? " came Clarissa's voice.

" It's Madame Glistanova," said her husband. " She wishes to call on you."

The door jerked open.

Clarissa, looking beautiful as a fashion plate, stood there holding in one hand her hat, a piled turbanesque model.

" Yes? " she said. " I was just trying to get this thing on so that it looks something like."

Xaria Glistanova smiled.

" In that case I shall not keep you long, my dear," she said. " But I did want to offer a word of congratulation on your performance this evening. Tosca is a long and tiring part and anyone who has sung it deserves praise."

Clarissa looked at her intently. The gallery was scarcely lit and it was difficult to make out people's expressions.

" And you came all the way up here to tell me that? " she said.

Madame Glistanova shrugged.

" It is not very far," she said.

G

Clarissa looked at her.

" Well, no," she answered, " not for someone with their health and strength. I dare say they could nip up in a couple of seconds. But don't say it wasn't an effort for you : those stairs are bloody steep."

Again Xaria Glistanova smiled.

" Then let them testify to the sincerity of my con-gratulations," she said.

" Yes," said Clarissa, " that's right."

She frowned puzzledly.

" But what I can't understand," she said, " is why you did it? Don't tell me I fooled you. You weren't even watching from the front, were you? "

" No, I was in the wings."

" Then you must have known. I mean, I can't get on with this acting business. But you, if what they say is true, you were one of the great ones. You used to sing Tosca, didn't you? "

" Yes, I sang Tosca."

" And at La Scala, wasn't it? "

" I sang it at La Scala, certainly."

" Then don't tell me you couldn't act. And that you didn't have a pretty terrific voice."

From behind Heinrich Einfalt interrupted.

" She was magnificent," he said. " The whole house gave her a standing ovation. It was a performance in a million."

Clarissa glanced at him briefly.

" Yes," she said, " that's what I supposed."

She turned again to Xaria Glistanova.

" So what's all this about congratulating me? " she said.

" You deserve congratulation. The part is a taxing one, and you sang it through."

Clarissa said nothing for a moment. She looked thoughtful and swung the tall hat by its ribbon.

" And you were just congratulating me on that? " she asked. " You were just congratulating me on getting through with it somehow? "

" It is no easy thing to do."

Clarissa smiled wryly.

" You're right enough there anyhow," she said.

Xaria Glistanova bowed slightly over her silver-headed stick and turned to go.

" All the same," said Clarissa suddenly, " you know I did better than just get through it."

Madame Glistanova continued to walk slowly along the gallery.

" Oh, yes, I did," said Clarissa. " Even though you don't think so. Oh, I know my acting's terrible, and my voice is only all right. I'll admit that to you, though I wouldn't to most people."

She stepped forward out of the doorway of her dressing-room fully on to the gallery.

" But I've got something I don't think even you had in your best days," she said loudly.

Xaria Glistanova stopped.

" I've got me," said Clarissa.

She stood straight in the half-light. She was uncontestably beautiful : and she had something else besides.

Her unrestrained ability to project an image of desirability.

" Yes," said Xaria Glistanova, " I am used to seeing

things from the singer's point of view. But now I can see that."

"And that's what the public can see," Clarissa said. "They can see it and they like it. I may not have the critics slobbering over my top notes, but you ask anyone in the streets of this town what they know about the Flinwich Festival. You know what they'll tell you? That I'm in it. Me."

She stood breathing deeply. The high line of her dress heaving.

"You know what the papers call me?" she said. "The voice with the body. And I'm proud about that. Damn' proud. I'm giving a hell of a lot of people just exactly what they want."

She swung round and went back into her dressing-room. Almost before she had crossed the threshold she was lifting up her tall, ridiculous hat and setting it firmly and easily on to her luxurious sweep of blonde hair.

Xaria Glistanova turned and walked slowly and with difficulty down the iron stairway to the stage.

Mrs. Craggs waited till she had reached the bottom and then set off to find an empty dressing-room to tackle.

On the stage the battlements of the Castle of Sant' Angelo had already disappeared. Stage hands were swarming everywhere. The set for the last act of *Death of A Fat God* was about to make its first appearance.

Don Francisco was the centre of all the turmoil. He rushed from one point to another. At one moment he was deep in energetic conversation with the stage director and in another had broken off and run over to the scene painter to launch into a flood of largely incomprehensible expostulation.

From the scene dock stage hands in pairs came walking forward with newly painted canvas flats wobbling high above their heads like carnival giants. Others like ants carried above themselves huge pieces of moulded fibreglass glitteringly decorated. Ropes from the flies swooped and dangled. Men stood patiently and pensively holding on to struts and stays with no one apparently ever ready to release them.

And through all the frenzy Xaria Glistanova and her little husband made their way. She walked forward slowly as ever but confidently, hardly bothering to keep an eye out for the huge bespangled pieces of scenery tottering past her.

She crossed the stage to the far side where under the gallery of men's dressing-rooms her husband had previously placed for her the ornate Italian chair at which Scarpia ate his supper. There she sat and waited while the scene for the final act of *Death of A Fat God* was laboriously brought to completion.

At last all was ready. The curious countryside that Prokovinski had conceived for the setting of his tale, an exhilarating blend of the classical and the oriental, had taken shape.

At one side of the stage there was the tree—half pastoral, half a wild jeweller's dream—under which the Goose Girl and the Shepherd were to sing their love. In the centre stood the temple dedicated to the cruel Fat God, a fantastic intermingling of Greece and India. In front of it was the space where the god's car, a cloud made by a goldsmith, would descend.

In twos and threes the stage hands departed and the

largely empty theatre was left to the small band who were to rehearse the opera's last act.

Paul Pivoine, who had appeared again without offering any explanation for his sudden departure when Xaria Glistanova had praised his playing, strode silently through the orchestra pit and took his seat at the ancient upright piano. Don Francisco abandoned the stage and went down to his usual place in the front row of the stalls.

The rehearsal began. It appeared to go well. Mary Arthur's silvery voice floated into the theatre as thrillingly as on the first occasion it had been heard there. Franz Prahler sitting by himself a few rows back in the stalls visibly puffed with pride at his pupil's success.

And then, just as a long aria came to an end, the thin black figure of Xaria Glistanova appeared out of the wings.

" Please," she said, " could we wait for one moment? "

She leant heavily forward on her stick as she waited for Don Francisco to answer.

" Yes, yes, certainly, Madame Glistanova," he said. " Every certainly. But all is going so well. Not for long to wait."

" It's because things are going so well that I wish to stop them," Xaria Glistanova said.

Her voice carried effortlessly into the dark auditorium.

She turned to Mary Arthur.

" You have a beautiful voice, my dear," she said. " Do not let it lead you astray."

Mary looked a little nettled. As well she might because she had been singing at her best and it was obvious from the expressions of the people round about that this was the general view.

" What do you mean? " she asked.

" That you are beginning to place too much reliance on the beauty of the voice alone," Xaria Glistanova said. " You are forgetting a little that it is not you singing, however beautifully, but it is the Goose Girl."

Mary shook her head and looked baffled.

" Well, I don't know about that," she said. " I'm singing the notes, aren't I? Perhaps if I was in the clothes or something you'd get a better idea of it."

Madame Glistanova smiled.

" The clothes would probably help you, my dear," she said. " But I do not need them. I have seen great acting in the most incongruous clothes and I can assure you that, if you too had watched it, you would have been in no doubt that it was not an actor or a singer standing there, but the very character they were representing."

Mary shrugged.

" Well," she said, " that's all very well for people who've been brought up to it. But till I was seventeen I'd never scarcely left the farm back in Australia. I can't start doing subtle stuff like that straight off. I'm singing the notes."

" Yes, you are singing the notes. You are singing them with great beauty."

" Then I reckon I'm doing all that anyone has a right to ask. If they wanted this European acting, then they ought to have got someone else to do the part. Though I bet they'd have found there's nothing like a voice brought up in the old outback for really putting it over."

Madame Glistanova turned to face the dark auditorium.

" I'm sorry to have interrupted, Don Francisco," she said. " I promise you it will not happen again."

Don Francisco bounced up from his seat.

" But please to do it always," he said. " Anythings what you says will be of the most great helps. Of the most great."

" Well, thank you," Xaria Glistanova said. " I will certainly do what I can."

She walked slowly back to Scarpia's chair in the deep gloom of the wings.

Paul returned to the music and for a little while the rehearsal proceeded smoothly. They reached once again the point where Jean-Artaban should descend in the god's car. And again there was a pause.

From up above them in the flies Jean-Artaban's voice came floating angrily down.

" Am I expected to step into this thing? It is not safe, I tell you."

Don Franciso ran his hands through his curly black hair.

" I come and explaining," he shouted. " It is most absolutely as safe as the bank."

He hurried across to the pass door and a moment later appeared on the stage. He stood near the back looking up into the darkness above and shading his eyes.

" Now, listen, Jean-Artaban," he shouted.

" There is no need to make all that noise, my good friend."

Don Francisco drew a long breath.

" I explaining," he said.

" I listening."

The parody was lost on the little Spaniard.

" You seeing the car, yes? "

" I see it. It is suspended on nothing."

"Exactly. This side of the set is nothings to be seen. But the floor of the car is on two thin steels. Yes?"

"I suppose you are right."

Don Francisco moved round on the stage still peering up trying to find a place from which he could see Jean-Artaban and gauge his reactions.

"So," he called up, "the steels go through two slittings in the flats. Yes, yes?"

"I can see two slits, certainly. I suppose you realise that the audience will be able to see them, too?"

"Not with the lightings and everythings."

"I shall believe that when I see it. However, that is your affair."

The shrug could be felt descending on to the stage from the darkness above.

"Then on the other side of the slittings is a platform with balance weights, and from this up going are the ropes."

Don Francisco was putting a good face on it.

"My dear friend," Jean-Artaban's voice came floating down, "you do not need to tell me the principle of this crazy machine. I can see it perfectly well for myself. And in any case you are almost totally incomprehensible."

Don Francisco was still undeterred.

"On the other end of the ropings——"

"On the other end of the ropes are weights equivalent to the weight of the car and the platform hidden from the audience, and with a small allowance for myself. So that in reality when I step on the machine there is only the smallest tendency to go down."

Jean-Artaban's lecturing tone was maddeningly pedantic.

" Yes. But you understanding all the time."

" Of course I understand, my friend. I am just question-whether the right ropes have been attached to the right weights. When I step into the car what will happen? "

" Nothing."

Don Francisco indulged in a complex gesture, which made things less clear than ever.

" Nothing," he repeated. " You see, the ropes will be helded by the brakings. Up in the gallery. Only when at the cueing the brakings are taken off will you descend."

" You do not understand, my friend," Jean-Artaban said. " If the brakes are on the wrong ropes, when I get into the car it will go down too soon. And if the weights are wrong it will go down so fast I will be killed."

" But that is not so."

" That I do not believe to begin with. And even if it is true, I know what has happened. Some fool has taken away the weights."

" But, no. That could not be so. On them is wroted a notice, ' Do Not Moving ' it say."

" And you think that makes everything safe? "

" Oh, yes. On none other weights in all the theatres is that wroted."

" And you think that is enough? "

" But yes, yes."

" But, no."

" But, yes."

It looked as if this slanging match with Don Francisco standing on the stage with his head thrust back as far as it would go and Jean-Artaban invisible in the darkness of the flies would go on and on for ever. But there came an interruption.

" You are quite right, Monsieur Pivoine."

It was Xaria Glistanova's voice.

She came on to the stage again and walked slowly across to Don Francisco.

" One cannot take too much trouble over this," she said. " In America when they tried to put on *Death of A Fat God* before there was terrible trouble over just such a machine. I remember thinking at the time that everybody was being foolish to worry, but not when I saw the car crash on to the stage."

Tears came into Don Francisco's eyes.

" I know there is troublings," he said. " But with me is not. I make sure all the time."

He looked round at the quite considerable group which had now gathered on the stage.

It was plain that his assertion was not being taken at its face value.

" Look," he shouted, glaring round at everybody. " I prove her."

He marched off the set in the direction of the iron stairway that led first to the fly gallery and then on up to the catwalk running out to the god's car hanging above them all.

Surreptitiously people made a wide circle round the place where the machine ought to land on the stage. At the back of the set there was a more pronounced scurry as people almost ran from the area on which the hidden platform would land.

" Ah, my good friend. . . ."

Jean-Artaban's voice greeting Don Francisco floated down.

" All right. Take off the brakings."

Don Francisco still sounded in a fury.

At the back of the fly gallery the two stagehands who had stayed behind to work the brakes looked at each other. One nodded. The other with his mouth tight shut slowly took off the levers.

CHAPTER IX

DON FRANCISCO floated gently down to the stage. The goldsmith's cloud god's car in which he stood came softly down in front of the set, while behind the set the heavy platform descended in parallel. Even without the final refinements of painting and lighting the two thin steel girders connecting car and platform were hard to see.

The descent in the end was so slow that Franz Prahler ran forward from his position of safety and irritably tugged the car down the last few inches to the floor.

" Well, *liebling*," he said, " certainly your trouble is not falling too fast."

Don Francisco, without answering, called back to the stage hands.

" Is the brakings on again? "

A muffled shout of reassurance came from behind the flats.

Don Francisco jumped out of the car.

" All the time I am tell you," he said. " Is as safe as housings."

He turned and called back again.

" Okay, take off the brakings again and let us see the car go up."

And promptly the car floated up into the darkness above.

"Well," said Mrs. Milhorne to Mrs. Craggs. "I reckon I'd better be getting along now. Heaven knows what my old man will say when I come in as late as this."

Her eyes gleamed momentarily in her pallid face as she buttoned her coat over her apron.

"It's funny, you know," she added, "I quite thought something awful was going to happen with that contrivance of theirs. And there it is, gone off as nicely as you could wish. Sort of what they call an anticlimax."

Mrs. Craggs looked at her.

"What did you expect then?" she said. "A fatality or something? Spoilt your evening, I dare say."

"I'm sure I never hope to see blood shed," Mrs. Milhorne replied with dignity. "I couldn't bear it, not with my temperament being what it is. But all the same I did expect something to happen."

::   ::

Once again the stage of the Flinwich Festival theatre was transformed a few days later into that fascinating concoction of classical restraint overlaid and wreathed round with wildly glittering oriental over-exuberance that is the hallmark of the exotic art of Prokovinski. For the second time the temple of the last act stood looking out in its forced harmony of pure white pillars and writhing porphyry ones ; at the flower-dotted greensward dominated by the jeweller's dream tree, half foliage and half ornament.

But on this occasion the small blemishes of the set's first trial had been almost totally removed. No longer was the temple sliced down by two thin black lines through which the steel supports of the god's car could slide. Final ingenious touches with a paint brush had placed discreet shadows on the canvas flats and a strategically placed spotlight had directed attention elsewhere. The slits were invisible from the stalls.

Down in the dark auditorium, where only the faintest sparkle showed where the huge chandelier hung above the sloping rows of empty seats, Mrs. Milhorne surveyed the new set with a keenly critical eye.

At last she turned to Mrs. Craggs sitting uncompromisingly hatted beside her.

" Well," she said, " I more see what they mean now. That first time I saw it, when they tried out the god's car, I must say I didn't think much of it. It seemed somehow not to blend together right. But it's come on a lot since they touched it up, it really has."

" I should hope so," Mrs. Craggs said. " If it wasn't looking all right for the dress rehearsal we should be in a pretty pickle."

" Yes," said Mrs. Milhorne, " and I think the whole thing's really lovely now. A bit what you might call bizarre like, and not to everyone's taste I dare say. But, for them as knows what the general idea is, it couldn't be better."

" Still, things have changed since it was first thought of," Mrs. Craggs said.

" Have they, dear ? "

" Yes. Didn't you know? "

" No. Can't say as I did."

Mrs. Milhorne frowned.

" How is it you always seem to know all about what's going on behind the scenes? " she asked.

A grim smile came fleetingly across Mrs. Craggs's face. " People are always ready to tell you things if they think you won't understand too much," she said.

Mrs. Milhorne looked at her sagely.

" I don't think that can be right, dear," she said. " It's the really understanding ones that get told things in my experience. And I should know. After all, if I'm not the understanding, sympathetic type I don't know who is. And you should hear the things that have been confided to me in my time."

Mrs. Craggs smiled again.

" Then you'll hear all about the peacocks business soon enough," she said.

Mrs. Milhorne tossed her head.

" All right," she said, " we all know you've been working here longer than what I have. If you want to take advantage, I'm sure you're welcome."

For half a minute Mrs. Craggs let her simmer in silence. Then she relented.

" I had it from Don Francisco himself in the first place," she said. " Very proud of his idea for them peacocks he was. Only he made the mistake of asking Madame Glistanova if Prokovinski has said anything about such a thing. Asked her right out in public, too."

" And did she tell him? "

" What do you think? "

" Well, I don't really know what to say."

" 'Course she told him," Mrs. Craggs said. " You can see the sort she is a mile off. If you ask her a question, she'll pay you the compliment of thinking you want to know the true answer. That was what made it so difficult for Don Francisco."

" How was that then? "

" Because he'd talked so much about having his real peacocks and all, and it turned out that someone had suggested them to Prokovinski and he'd just looked at them and laughed out loud. So Don Francisco had to forget he'd ever got the peacocks."

" You mean to say he'd actually got them? "

Mrs. Milhorne was so surprised she conceded a point before she had even thought about it.

Mrs. Craggs generously provided a spate of information without being further pressed.

" Yes," she said, " got 'em and got 'em for good, I reckon. He can't get rid of 'em it seems. The place where he bought them was only too glad to get shot of 'em. Couldn't stand the screeching."

She chuckled.

" Know where they are now? " she said.

And without waiting for Mrs. Milhorne to fish for the reply she told her.

" They're the official responsibility of the stage door-keeper," she said. " Old Strutt's been put in charge of them. They were in his room half one morning. Four of 'em. Made a nasty mess they did, too. And now he's got 'em out at his allotment. He was foolish enough to tell Don Francisco he'd got an empty hen run out there. Thought to curry a bit of favour, I dare say."

Her eyes under the square line of her hat gleamed.

" The people in the neighbourhood are kicking up a rare fuss from what I hear," she went on. " Being woken at six of a morning with the blessed things squawking and screaming. They say they'll go to the council about it if something's not done soon. Abatement of a nuisance they call it."

She laughed.

" Well, perhaps that was the cause of it," said Mrs. Milhorne thoughtfully.

" The cause of what, dear? "

" What happened to me when I happened to pop into Mr. Strutt's box one morning," said Mrs. Milhorne. " I was just going to pass the time of day a bit, but his temper was so frayed I had to leave."

Mrs. Craggs chuckled.

" Got your head bit off good and proper, I dare say."

" Well, he certainly wasn't at all polite. But further than that I'm not prepared to go."

" I'll imagine it, dear. Anyhow, that's how it came about that Don Francisco wanted someone to tell his troubles to. He had to make out to somebody that he wasn't wrong but had just had second thoughts on the subjects of peacocks in general like. And when he happens to find me in his office doing a bit of dusting, he must have thought I was just what he was looking for."

Mrs. Milhorne drew herself up.

" I'm surprised that he thought you were the one to confide in, dear," she said.

" 'Course I was the one. He thought I wouldn't realise the truth. Nobody ever wants to confide in a judge. What they want is a nice simple old body they can make believe whatever they say."

" Well, I must say I wouldn't like to tell my troubles to one of them lynx-eyed sort that's always picking holes in everything you say."

" I'm sure you wouldn't, dear."

H

Mrs. Milhorne looked at the auditorium dotted here and there with people whose business it was to watch the dress rehearsal.

" Take that Madame Glistanova now," she said. " You were mentioning only a moment ago the way she will always tell you a bit more than you'd bargained for. I wouldn't care for that."

" Then you should take care not to ask her questions, dear. Fancy going up to her and wanting to know if she thought it mattered singers being in tune."

" Well, I was interested, that's all. And I must say I never realised till she told me in that sharp way of hers that so many real singers on the stage were off the note. I felt quite encouraged for a bit until she got on to that about how the public ought to hiss them off. I shouldn't like that."

" What were you encouraged about? " said Mrs. Craggs.

" Oh, nothing, dear, nothing. Just something I thought about."

" Hm."

" I tell you one thing though," Mrs. Milhorne plunged on, " I can't never understand how she came to marry him."

" What, Xaria Glistanova marry that little Mr. Einfalt? " Mrs. Craggs said.

" Yes. And him such a nice gentleman. 'Course I see how it was with him in a way. It was something he said once that put me on to it. About her refusing to marry three crowned heads. Do you think it was true? "

" From all I hear it was. I can't say I'm much surprised."

" But crowned heads. And three. You'd have thought she'd get wore down."

" Wore down? Her? It'd take more than three crowned heads to wear that one down."

" Yes, I dare say you're right. She's hard. There's no denying it. Hard as nails. And him so nice and gentle. Still, you can see how he must have felt. To be the one chosen above kings."

" Yes," said Mrs. Craggs, " you can see how he must have felt."

Mrs. Milhorne nodded in solemn agreement.

" Oh," she said, " I spotted the remark at once. It sort of gave me a key to the understanding of his innermost nature, as you might say. Mind you, I'm like that. See to the depths of people in a flash I do. Even my old man remarks on it."

" It wouldn't take much of a flash to see to the innermost depths of him," Mrs. Craggs said.

" Well, that's as may be. Still, I hope you never hear me defending him in public."

For a little Mrs. Milhorne contemplated her domestic life.

" Well," she said eventually, " I wouldn't mind having him as a husband, I can tell you that."

" What, him? " said Mrs. Craggs.

" Yes, him. A real gentleman if ever there was one. None of that ugly pushing and always wanting to have his own way."

Mrs. Craggs looked down the length of the auditorium at the dome-shaped head of Heinrich Einfalt sitting one seat removed from the thin elegant silhouette of his wife.

" No," she said, " none of that pushing. Not even

enough to push himself through life. You can have him, dear."

Down in the orchestra pit, now filled with musicians, Boscani tapped his three impatient taps on the top of his music stand.

Mrs. Milhorne ostentatiously turned and gave her full attention to the stage.

The rehearsal went well. Mary Arthur's voice was if anything more astonishing than ever. It seemed to light up the darkened auditorium in a cascade of silver.

Franz Prahler, too, was in good form, encouraged by the evident success of his protégée. Margherita Clarone appeared equally to promise well for the first night. Although her voice could not compare in quality with the extraordinary clear brilliance and agility of Mary's or the well-loved golden tones of Franz, she nevertheless was singing at her best and the furious tirades of the Harpy gave her exactly the acting opportunities at which she excelled.

Even Jean-Artaban refrained from spoiling the occasion. Stimulated by the splendid singing of the others he concentrated instead on giving what he thought was his best. And if this was brutally unsubtle the immense power of his voice, combined with a natural beastliness of character which crossed the footlights like a bomb, made his performance decidedly worth watching.

There was hardly a single hitch. At one point a minor production muddle came to light and Mary Arthur found herself prevented from getting to the right place to make her final entrance at the right time. But with shouts of " Not mattering, not mattering," Don Francisco insisted that the performance should go on despite this trouble.

It ran on to the final curtain almost as smoothly as before. There was some slight mechanical difficulty over the descent of the god's car, but even over this Jean-Artaban created no trouble. High and low there was a feeling of warm self-satisfaction.

After the hubbub of excited congratulation had died down Don Francisco called out that he would like Mary, Margherita, Franz and Jean-Artaban to wait behind to iron out the two difficulties that had arisen. One by one the numerous body of people concerned with the opera departed to go to their beds. Only the youngest and most innocent of the stagehands was left behind to operate the god's car in the final run-through.

Boscani had a last conference with Don Francisco, who assured him that Paul Pivoine's services as pianist would be quite adequate, and then he left on the heels of the orchestra, throwing good wishes out behind him like a flower girl on a carnival float.

Don Francisco went and leant against the rail of the orchestra pit and discussed the music with Paul. Jean-Artaban appeared on the stage and looked at his son with obvious contempt. But as Don Francisco did not notice him he turned with a heavy shrug and made his way backstage through the temple entrance at about the point where he was accustomed to descend in his god's car.

Suddenly the lazy silence of the big, deserted theatre was broken by a sharp voice.

"Look, I warned you. You didn't take any notice. Well, that's too bad for you."

CHAPTER X

THE AUSTRALIAN ACCENT was unmistakable.

Mary Arthur.

Both Don Francisco and Paul looked up. Don Francisco shrugged, but looked worried. Paul stayed for some seconds staring without expression at the pillared temple entrance through which his father had just disappeared. Then suddenly he brushed past the little Spanish director and strode down into the tunnel out of the pit.

A moment or two later both he and Mary came out through the temple on to the stage. Paul was talking to her in a low voice and she seemed to be trying to lighten the situation. She laughed quietly and smiled up at the sullen young pianist.

Mrs. Craggs and Mrs. Milhorne, carrying their brooms and dustpans, crossed the stage from the " gentlemen's side " to the " ladies' side."

Don Francisco called up to Mary.

" Are you ready, my dear? We will beginning."

Mary left Paul.

" Yes," she said, " ready whenever you are."

" Then the others must be coming on to the stage. I will tell them what must be do."

" I'll call them."

Mary went over to the temple and called through it.

" Jean-Artaban, Jean-Artaban. We're beginning."

There seemed to be no constraint in her way of shouting his name. But it was difficult to see whom else she could have been speaking to with almost hysterical fierceness just a few moments before.

In an instant Jean-Artaban appeared. With him now was his wife.

She came at once to the footlights and leant forward to address Don Francisco.

" I guess I really shouldn't be here," she said. " I know all you people have a lot of work to do. But I absolutely insist on driving Jean-Artaban home. He believes that there are never any other cars out at night and drives right in the middle of the road."

" It is where I like to drive," said Jean-Artaban equably.

" Well, dear, it's where you'll hit someone else one of these nights," Alice said. " But not if I can help it."

" But, dear madam," said Don Francisco, " you are always the most welcome."

Behind Alice a small group had collected on the stage. Besides Jean-Artaban and Mary, there was Franz and Margherita and the sole callow stagehand who had been left to operate the car, as well as Xaria Glistanova and Heinrich Einfalt. The last bowed two or three times to Don Francisco but without being noticed.

" If we can be of any assistance," he lisped at last. " There was much the same trouble about this entrance of the Goose Girl when Prokovinski was there to supervise the production."

He bowed again.

" But Madame Glistanova's helping is always the most good to have," Don Francisco said.

" The trouble is," said Xaria Glistanova, " that Prokovinski was not thinking of a real stage at all when he wrote this part. There isn't, in point of fact, enough time for the Goose Girl to get round to the temple entrance after she has made her exit by the tree."

Don Francisco looked relieved.

" I am thinking that," he said.

" So what we did was to repeat some of the music. Let me see the score and I will show you."

Don Francisco hurried round through the pass door and up on to the stage clasping the large green-bound volume of the score. He went over to Xaria Glistanova and they plunged into a heavy technical discussion.

The others chatted in a desultory fashion. After the excitement of the successful dress rehearsal they were beginning to feel a bit flat.

The only exception was the never deflated Franz. He bounced about in front of the little group perfectly cheerfully.

" Well, *lieblings*," he said, " on the night we will have a great success."

Nobody responded.

" Do you know what it will bring me? " Franz asked.

Again nobody seemed very interested.

But Franz was not easily daunted.

" It will bring me precisely nothing," he said.

Alice Pivoine rose at this like a lazy fish coming to the surface of a summer pond.

" Don't tell me you've agreed to sing without fee? " she said.

Franz laughed.

" Without fee, no," he said. " But such a fee as they are able to pay. Pfui. In taxes it will all go."

" Not unless you're in a very unusual position with the

fiscal authorities," Alice said. " It is just possible that by earning more you put yourself just on the wrong side of a higher tax bracket and actually have less to spend. But it's very unlikely."

Franz shook his head like a dog emerging from a stream.

" Tax, figures, sums," he said. " I do not understand them. To deal with all that I have accountants. But of this I am sure. I sing at Flinwich for fame only. If I wanted to make money I would do a film."

Alice seemed determined not to let him get out of it.

" Too bad if you woke up in the morning with a cold," she said. " Then the critics wouldn't hear you and there'd be no fame for Franzie."

" Colds, colds," Franz said, bobbing up like a ball pushed under water. " I never have colds. I lead always a healthy life. I drink good wine and eat plenty of good food. Do you know something? "

He turned and advanced towards the little group as if he had a really startling piece of information to impart.

" Do you know something, *lieblings*? Every morning I get out of bed and straight away without doing anything else I sing a long high G. How about that? "

Jean-Artaban closed his eyes.

Dissatisfied with this response Franz harked back to an earlier theme.

" But I sometimes wonder why I came here at all," he said. " Because, you know, what do I care for the critics? "

He looked at the others. They did not appear to be greatly shocked.

" No," Franz said, " it is not the critics I care about.

It is the little people who write to me. Every day the pile
of letters. The thanks for bringing beauty into their
lives."

"Together with the contracts from the little impresarios," Alice added.

"But those too make me proud," said Franz. "If the
public did not want me to make great concert tours then
the impresarios would not send me the contracts. The
contracts just show how the public loves me. The bigger
the contract, the more the love."

"It would not be difficult to make immense sums singing the sort of thing you do," Jean-Artaban said.

He spoke with less than his usual conviction. He must
have known that Franz had an answer.

"Ach, no, *liebling*," Franz burst in eagerly, "do not
think you can make me ashamed of the songs I sing. They
touch the people. They have true lyricism, they make
more people happy than any opera ever did in all the
world. Of that I am proud. But—— "

He held up his hand to command attention as if an
eager chorus of dissent had broken out.

It palpably had not.

"But," he repeated, "do not think that I, myself, do
not equally appreciate opera. Even Prokovinski."

He shook his head.

"You do not believe me, *liebling*? But there are the
critics to prove me right. 'Herr Prahler sang with such
sensitivity. . . .' 'Mr. Prahler sang with all the accom-
plished musicianship. . . .' You can read them by the
hundred."

Jean-Artaban smiled lugubriously.

"Nevertheless," he said, "some of us have made not

inconsiderable sums by singing operas one cannot be ashamed of."

A jibe at the type of musical entertainment that had made Franz so famous had no effect on him, but the implication that someone else was as financially successful as himself went home.

" In Bavaria," he snapped, " I have a *schloss*."

" In the Loire I have a château," retorted Jean-Artaban.

His wife took a couple of paces forward so that she was more or less standing between him and the bouncy Franz.

" Oh, come, Jean-Artaban," she said, " it may be a château in name but it's just dinky."

" In my *schloss*," Franz said, " there are thirty rooms."

" And in my château thirty-three."

" If you count the johns," Alice interrupted.

" But such places are rooms," Franz said. " When my *schloss* was built they were not made as lavatories, so it is right to count them as rooms still. For tax they are counted. So much I have to pay each year."

" Yes," said Alice, " I guess Jean-Artaban shares that problem too. It's one I've heard about. To my cost."

Jean-Artaban looked at her gloomily. No doubt he could have wished that the immensity of his taxes had been more sympathetically presented.

His gloom was quickly added to. Margherita had begun to take an interest in the conversation. If her former husband was being baited she was not going to be left out.

" Ah," she said, " that château, how well I remember it. It was always Jean-Artaban's bribe for his mistresses. Is it still the same, madame? "

" Well," Alice replied, totally unperturbed, " if I knew the answer to that it would be ' no ', wouldn't it? "

" But it is not," Jean-Artaban stormed. " My heart is not easily captured, but once it is caught it is caught for life."

" With periods of parole," Margherita said quickly.

Jean-Artaban turned to her, his face reddening with rage.

" You are thinking my heart was captured by you? " he said. " Then you are thinking wrong. No wonder I had mistresses when you were my wife. It is only surprising I did not need a harem to console myself."

" Oh, it was to console yourself," Margherita said. " It was not to indulge yourself in pleasures, I suppose? Is that what you have mistresses for now? "

" I have no mistresses now. I swear it."

Margherita smiled slowly. Something to savour.

" Yes, Jean-Artaban," she said, " I believe you. I believe you entirely. You have no mistresses now."

" It is as well for you that you told the truth then," Jean-Artaban said darkly. " I know how to pay you out."

" Yes, you know how to pay me out. And you know how to pay your mistresses off. Like you have just paid off that poor Clarissa Glass."

Margherita stood looking at her ex-husband with a wonderfully fierce expression.

She held it.

It was the expression she was most proud of.

She was still holding it, and the others in the group were beginning to steal glances at Alice to see how Margherita's revelation had affected her, when from the orchestra pit Don Francisco called briskly out to them.

" Please, please, please. We are now readying. Please take the place for the scene from the beginning of No. 87."

Everybody considered it easiest to comply with his request without attempting to prolong their conversation.

Only Alice had a last word.

" Listen, Jean-Artaban, honey," she said, " you be good now. None of your tricks this once. I want the rehearsal to finish just as soon as possible, so we can go home to bed."

A claim asserted.

So without Jean-Artaban's wife hearing of the way in which her husband had dismissed Clarissa, a piece of gossip universally considered too hot to handle, the cast went to their places for the last rehearsal of all. Jean-Artaban climbed like a great bear up to get to the catwalk next to his golden cloud car. Mary Arthur went and sat beneath the bejewelled tree under which she was to sing her duet with Franz. Margherita crossed to the other side of the stage to deliver the Harpy's curse that made the duet into a trio. Alice, Xaria Glistanova and her husband moved discreetly into the dark wings near the corridor leading to the stage door. The young stagehand, struck doubly dumb by the presence of so many stars, went up to his row of brakes at the back of the fly gallery.

Don Francisco hurried round to his customary seat in the first row of the dark auditorium. As soon as he had arrived he called to Paul at the battered rehearsal piano and Paul began to play.

In Clarissa Glass's dressing-room Mrs. Milhorne, who had summoned Mrs. Craggs from her work in the room next door to help her move the singer's heavy trunk, stopped and set the trunk down. She cocked an ear towards the sound of the piano.

" This bit always makes me feel sort of queer," she said.

She sat down on the trunk.

" It's that long part with the Goose Girl singing and no accompaniment that does it," said Mrs. Craggs. " There's a lot to be said for a composer with sense enough to write as little music as necessary."

" I dare say you're right," Mrs. Milhorne conceded. " Not but what I'm not partial to a drop of orchestral colour meself."

Down in the orchestra pit Paul played on. Prokovinski's exotic, fantastic music rolled out.

On the stage the rehearsal went smoothly. Mary and Franz sang their duet half-voice. Margherita joined in for the trio. She left. Franz sang his one last long golden note and left in his turn. Mary finished the duet on stage alone. Then she, too, made her exit.

Paul played on, came to the repeat which Xaria Glistanova had suggested, and played it. It seemed to provide ample time for Mary to get round from the exit by the tree to the temple entrance from just inside which she was to sing her long unaccompanied passage before her final entrance and the imminent descent of the Fat God.

" Sing it, sing it, please."

Don Francisco's voice came excitedly up from the darkness of the auditorium.

Mary sang.

Up in Clarissa's dressing-room Mrs. Craggs had left in despair to get on with her own work. Mrs. Milhorne was still sitting open-mouthed on the trunk.

She sighed deeply.

" A real lovely voice," she said to herself.

And in mid-phrase with the suddenness of a wireless brutally switched off, the voice stopped.

There was a dull, heavy thudding sound. And utter silence.

CHAPTER XI

LOOKING DOWN from the ironwork fly gallery, Mrs. Craggs could see at once what had happened.

Through the gap in the scenery which from the auditorium looked like the temple entrance a thick swath of bright light fell. It illuminated the darkness on either side. And in this pool of light it was very easy to see the heavy platform which balanced behind the scenes the god's car in front.

It was lying almost on the stage.

Almost but not quite.

Its fall had been checked by the body of Mary Arthur. The thin costume of the Goose Girl emphasised the look of entire defencelessness.

Even from the distance at which Mrs. Craggs was looking there could be no doubt that the heavy platform had killed the little Australian girl instantly.

Mrs. Craggs turned and ran along the gallery to the iron stairway leading down to the stage.

The sound of her heavy shoes banging their way down without ceremony seemed to startle the rest of the theatre into life. Mrs. Milhorne came out of Clarissa's dressing-room, saw Mary's body and began to scream. From the darkness on the other side of the stage four figures emerged

—Franz from his dressing-room, Alice from her husband's, Xaria Glistanova and Heinrich Einfalt from the deep shadows under the fly gallery. From high in the flies above them all a deep voice shouted out.

"What has happened? The car has descended. I can't see what it has done."

It was Jean-Artaban.

Before Mrs. Craggs had reached the stage there was the sound of running feet and Don Francisco and Paul appeared from the front of the house.

Everybody ran forward. But three or four yards from Mary's body they stopped and stood in an awed semi-circle looking at the girl who instants before had been singing in the empty theatre with a fine-spun beauty of tone that they had all expected to astonish the world.

It was left to Mrs. Craggs to go forward, kneel with difficulty and touch the body.

"She's dead. Dead, poor kid," she said.

And all the while above them on the gallery of the ladies' side dressing-rooms Mrs. Milhorne went on screaming. A thin, watery wailing sound going on and on.

Slowly Mrs. Craggs got to her feet.

"There's nothing we can do for the poor kid," she said. "She must have been standing just where the counter-balance platform would come down, but I wonder——"

She broke off and looked up angrily at Mrs. Milhorne.

"I wish to God somebody would stop her doing that," she said.

But already somebody had decided to deal with Mrs. Milhorne.

Xaria Glistanova was ascending the iron staircase of the

gallery, following the same route as she had taken not long before when she had gone to congratulate Clarissa Glass on her performance as Tosca. And this time she was managing without the aid of her husband or of Mrs. Craggs at the top of the stair.

She walked, bent forward a little from the hips, along the gallery until she reached Mrs. Milhorne. Then she raised her thin right arm, quietly and deliberately, and slapped Mrs. Milhorne across the face with all the force she could muster.

It was enough.

Mrs. Milhorne's screaming ceased.

Jean-Artaban came down the stairs from the flies above, paused for a moment on a level with Madame Glistanova and Mrs. Milhorne, looked at them expressionlessly and went on down. In the heavy jewel-encrusted robes of the Fat God with a circlet of nodding purple plumes above his head he looked obscenely out of place.

Not until he got to the stage did he speak.

"I always told you the car was dangerous," he said. "I might have been in it."

His wife gave a little moan.

"But, Jean-Artaban," she said, "why weren't you? It must have been nearly time for your entrance."

"I always knew it was dangerous," Jean-Artaban said.

It was not clear whether he was offering this as an explanation or whether he was simply dazedly repeating his first reaction.

Franz, in the incongruous tunic of the Shepherd, looked down at Mary's body.

"Such a voice, such a voice," he crooned. "Such a voice, and now it is gone."

I

"We shall have to cancel the performancings," Don Francisco said.

Suddenly Paul burst into noisy sobbing. The sound was not pleasant, heavy, gulping and catarrhal.

An epitaph.

After a little his father took a couple of paces towards him.

"Stop that noise," he said. "Stop it. What was she to you particularly? Do you think you are the only person here? Others have been affected by this tragedy without making fools of themselves."

Slowly Paul's sobs faded out.

As they did so, Mrs. Craggs suddenly turned from her silent contemplation of the broken body of Mary Arthur.

"Of course," she said, "where is he? Something drove it right out of my head."

"Where is who? Please talk sense," Jean-Artaban snapped.

"The young chap on the brakes," Mrs. Craggs said. "I thought at the time they were chancing their arm a bit leaving him on his own to manage the whole thing. And now look what's happened. Where is he?"

They all turned and looked up at the back of the fly gallery where the row of brake levers stood. In the back-stage gloom it was difficult to make anything out.

Mrs. Craggs went across to the iron stairway leading up to the gallery. Quickly she climbed up. When she turned to look along towards the brakes a sharp gasp came from her lips.

"What is it? What is it?" Alice called out from below.

Mrs. Craggs ran forward.

The stout shoes clanked hollowly on the iron grid of the back gallery. When she got to the brakes she stooped quickly.

" He's not there, is he? He's not dead, too? " Alice called.

Suddenly Mrs. Craggs laughed.

The harsh, unexpected sound.

She got to her feet wincing when the jab of pain came in her stiff hip joint.

" No," she said, " he's not dead. I thought he must have been when I spotted him lying there. But he isn't."

She looked down at the young stagehand.

" He's fainted," she said.

Slowly she knelt again, taking care this time to go down in the way she knew her hip joint tolerated best. She began tapping at the sallow face of the stagehand with sharp blows of her work-hardened hands.

It was not long before he groaned.

" Sit up now," Mrs. Craggs said.

The boy groaned again and hoisted himself half-way up.

" Now," said Mrs. Craggs, " what happened? "

" Happ—— Oh, my God, has something terrible happened? "

The boy began dragging himself to his feet.

" Well," said Mrs. Craggs, " you'll have to know sooner or later. I dare say it's best to tell you straight away. Mary Arthur is dead, lad."

The boy looked at her. Even in the poor light she could see that his face was terribly white.

" The platform hit her? " he asked.

" I'm afraid it did. What did you do? "

" Nothing. I tell you I didn't do nothing. The whole

thing suddenly began to go. I swear I never even touched the brakes."

Mrs. Craggs pushed past him unceremoniously. She looked at the brake levers.

The boy was right. They were still fully applied.

Mrs. Craggs bent forward and peered closely at the clean, new ropes stretched tautly in the dim light. Here and there on them were slight scorch marks.

She turned to the white-faced boy.

" You didn't do anything, lad," she said. " But I tell you what somebody else did : they took off the weights down below. With those gone no brakes on earth could hold the full weight of all that contraption."

She looked down over the rail of the fly gallery at the heavy counterbalance platform. It completely blotted out from this view the crushed body of the little Australian.

" I'd better go and ask Strutt at the stage door to phone for the police," she called down.

Nobody replied.

" Well," she said, " the police ought to be got and I'm going to ask Strutt to phone through."

She clumped down the iron stairs and went across to the corridor going down to the stage door. At the far end of it she found Mr. Strutt, the stage doorkeeper, sitting perched on a tall stool in the depths of his narrow room with his chin on the topmost silver button on his uniformed chest.

" Mr. Strutt."

Mrs. Craggs's voice had a note of sharp asperity.

" What's this? " Mr. Strutt shouted angrily. " What the hell do you want? "

" I want the police," Mrs. Craggs said grimly. " Mary Arthur's dead."

" Dead? What do you mean, dead? "

Mr. Strutt had a boiled face at the best of times and a bristly moustache. Now he was angry his face almost shone as if it had been lit from within and his moustache looked as if at any moment it would shoot off at Mrs. Craggs hair by hair in rapid fire.

" I mean the god's car thing crashed on her," Mrs. Craggs said.

She took no notice of Mr. Strutt's super-evident rage.

" Then what she needs is a doctor, a doctor," Mr. Strutt said.

He appeared hardly able to get the words out.

" She's past needing a doctor. Just you get on to the police."

" But what the hell have the police go to do with it? "

" They've got plenty to do with it, my lad. At the least there's been an accident through a very nasty piece of carelessness, but, if you ask me, there's been more than that. There's been a murder."

::   ::

" Well," said Mrs. Milhorne next morning, " I don't like to think there could be anything nasty like that, especially in an opera house."

Mrs. Craggs sniffed.

" It's bad enough the poor thing passing on like that," Mrs. Milhorne added, " without any suggestions of that sort."

Mrs. Craggs flashed her a scornful glance.

" Passing on."

" And another thing," said Mrs. Milhorne, " I don't

know as how they ought to have closed the theatre for to-night. They ought to have put on something else. Something a bit cheerful. I mean, the poor thing's gone and we ought to try to forget it if we can."

"You won't forget her in a hurry," Mrs. Craggs said.

"And why not I should like to know."

"Because she didn't just pass on. She was murdered. And there'll be police and reporters and heaven knows what here till you've had more than enough of them."

"Murdered."

Mrs. Milhorne tossed her head.

"You wait," said Mrs. Craggs. "You wait till the police ask to talk to you, that's all. Then you'll know whether it's murder or not. Nothing but questions about did you hear Miss Arthur having rows with anybody or anything. I know : I had the beginnings of it last night."

Mrs. Milhorne's eyes had brightened a little.

"You mean rows with any other singers? " she asked.

"With anybody at all."

"I don't think they'll regret coming to me," Mrs. Milhorne said. "If they want to know something about what goes on here, they'll find I'm the right person."

She rested her broom against the wall.

"It's the way I see into people, in a blinding flash," she said.

Mrs. Craggs continued methodically to sweep away at her half of the foyer.

"Still," she said, "if you're so sure it was only an accident, it won't matter what you think of anybody, will it? "

"Well," said Mrs. Milhorne, "it isn't up to me exactly to say. I mean, if the police think they should know exactly how people got on with that poor girl, then I think I should tell them."

For a little while she watched Mrs. Craggs sweeping.

"But what I can't understand is," she said, "why there's been all this talk of murder. The god's car just fell down, didn't it? I can't see why everyone should think it was done on purpose."

"It's quite simple," Mrs. Craggs said. "The car was held up by weights on the end of the ropes. Somebody took 'em off."

"It could have been a mistake, couldn't it? We can't all go through life without making mistakes."

"I suppose it might have been a mistake. But it looks precious unlikely. I should think everybody must have known the weights had to be left there. Look what a fuss Jean-Artaban kept making about them. And there was a plain warning notice on them, too. I saw it dozens of times myself."

"Well," said Mrs. Milhorne, "I don't understand this mechanical business. I'm more the artistic type, as you might say."

"It doesn't need much understanding."

Mrs. Craggs swept grimly on.

"No," she said, "what really kept the car up was the weights. The ropes came from the counterbalance platform, went up over pulleys, down past the brakes and ended up under the fly gallery at the weights. The brakes couldn't hold the thing once those weights had gone."

"But what exactly are the weights? I can't say I ever specially noticed them."

"They're just weights. As the car goes down they go up."

Mrs. Milhorne frowned.

" But how can they be taken off? "

" It's easy enough. They're round iron things looking like so many fruit cakes, if you know what I mean. Only they each have a slit in them, like as if you'd taken out a slice only not tapering it off towards the middle."

" Yes," said Mrs. Milhorne, " I can see that. Just as if it was my own baking."

" Well," Mrs. Craggs said, " on the end of the rope where you want to put the weights you have an iron bar and they just slip on to it. You put on just as many as you need to get the balance right."

" I see," said Mrs. Milhorne.

She did not sound altogether happy.

" And somebody slipped 'em off," said Mrs. Craggs. " They could have done it quite easy. One tip and they'd go."

Mrs. Milhorne sighed.

" Well," she said, " I don't understand, and that's a fact."

Mrs. Craggs had finished her half of the foyer. She pushed her pile of dust into Mrs. Milhorne's half.

" I'll leave you to gather it all up, dear," she said, " seeing as how you seem to be the last to-day."

Mrs. Milhorne looked at her.

" Well," she said, " what if the police want to see me. There's more important things than sweeping floors, you know. There's murder."

" Murder or no murder," Mrs. Craggs said, taking her coat off the hook on which she had hung it when she began on the foyer, " there's dirt, and it's got to be swept up."

She buttoned her coat tightly round herself and left Mrs. Milhorne alone in the partly swept foyer looking sadly at the pile of dust.

CHAPTER XII

DON FRANCISCO came into his office like a fox reaching its earth at last.

Mrs. Craggs, busy dusting the top of one of the large abstract canvases that decorated the walls, began to climb down from the Swedish-styled chair on which she had been standing.

" I'm sorry, sir," she said, " I thought you were out and I was just taking the chance to give the room a bit of a turn-out. I couldn't get in earlier with all them policemen about."

" Soon they will be work in here," Don Francisco said. " You stay and finishing what you do."

He stood beside his sleek ebony desk watching her gloomily as she climbed back up on to the Swedish chair.

" Tell me something, Mrs. Cragg," he said.

" Craggs, if you don't mind, sir."

" I am sorries. But, tell me, what do you think about all this businesses? "

" I don't know that it's my part to think, sir."

Don Francisco went round his desk and sat down.

" I have had to cancelling *Death of A Fat God*," he said.

" Well, I suppose you couldn't do nothing else," said Mrs. Craggs.

Don Francisco sighed.

" I would like to cancelling all the other performance,"
he said.

Mrs. Craggs climbed down from the abstract canvas
and started attacking a piece of primitive African sculp-
ture on top of a filing cabinet.

" I don't think that would go down too well," she said.

" Are you certains? "

Don Francisco sounded disappointed.

" Well, sir, people are at last beginning to like opera
in Flinwich, especially the popular ones as you might say."

" You don't think they would have liked *Death of A Fat
God*? "

" Not much."

" I do not like *Tosca* and *Rigoletto* too much. They are
not works that need great productioning."

" No, I can see that."

Flick, flick, flick went the duster.

" All the same," Mrs. Craggs said, " *Tosca* and *Rigoletto* are the operas people like. I mean, that's what old
Mr. Creassels left his money for : to get people in Flinwich liking opera. And *Tosca* is opera all right."

Don Francisco leaned earnestly forward over the ebony
desk.

" But Mrs. Cragg—Mrs. Craggs, is very simple. Tell
me, please, don't you thinking *Tosca* is too simple? "

" I'm sure I don't know, sir. It suits me pretty well.
It's not much like life, I know, but it's more so than
Death of A Fat God, if you take my meaning."

" Yes."

Don Francisco fell silent.

Mrs. Craggs finished the dusting.

" Well," she said, " I must be getting along."

" Mrs. Craggs, people would be very angry if I end the Flinwich Festival because of the murder? "

" They would, sir."

" But it would be respecting for the dead."

" No one in Flinwich knew Miss Arthur, nice girl though she was, sir. It's quite enough to cancel *Death of A Fat God*."

" I have to doing that : only one person in the world is meant to be able to sing that part. And when Madame Da Costa-O'Brien left I was already too lucky to get Mary Arthur. Now is no one left possibly."

" Well, you can count it as a gesture of respect all the same. But if you took away the operas people down here have got to like, there'd be such an outcry you'd never hear the end of it."

" So the festival goes on to the finishing."

A doleful statement of fact.

" I never expected you'd say anything else, sir."

" No."

Don Francisco regarded the shining surface of the ebony desk.

Mrs. Craggs made for the door.

" But who is this Superintendent Pryde? "

At Don Francisco's question Mrs. Craggs stopped.

" Did you say Superintendent Pryde, sir? "

" I sometimes not good at catching English names."

" Still, you know who he is, don't you? "

" I am ask."

" He's the bloke they call Pryde of the Yard in the papers. He's the real top-notch murder-squad man. They say he's ' The Man Who Never Fails.' Is he coming down here? "

" Already he is here. He is come to see me in just a few minutes."

" Well, I must say. Fancy us having a murder that they send him down for. The papers will be fuller of it than ever."

" The papers, the papers."

Don Francisco looked up with a wild grimace.

" The papers of *Death of A Fat God* they make insults. They say ' a weirdie opera.' It is not fair-play. And be looking."

He snatched his brief-case up and tugged out of it the whole batch of the morning's papers. Feverishly he began searching through them to inflict upon himself once again the various unflattering ways their crime reporters had chosen to describe *Death of A Fat God*.

Mrs. Craggs stood politely watching.

But before Don Francisco had had time to assemble the evidence to his own masochistic desire there came a sharp rap on the door.

Don Francisco took no notice.

He continued busily flipping open the papers, piling them up, losing the ones he had selected and beginning again.

The rap was repeated. Still Don Francisco was absorbed.

" There's someone at the door I do believe," said Mrs. Craggs. " Shall I let them in, sir? "

" Looking," said Don Francisco, " here it is : ' a barmy, beatnik beanfeast '."

He jabbed an indignant finger down on the offending phrase.

" I'll let them in then," said Mrs. Craggs.

She put a token hint of a question into the sentence even though she knew it would go quite unrecognised.

But before her hand had reached the doorknob the door was jerked open.

A tall man with broad shoulders and a large, strongly-featured face came striding into the room.

He took a quick glance round from under his jutting black eyebrows.

"Good morning," he said. "My name is Pryde, Detective Superintendent Pryde, Scotland Yard. I thought I heard voices so I took the liberty of coming in."

He turned back to the doorway.

"Jenkins," he said.

A shorter man with a resolutely non-committal expression presented himself.

"Come in, Jenkins," Superintendent Pryde said.

He turned back to Don Francisco.

"Detective-Sergeant Jenkins, my assistant," he said.

Don Francisco blinked at them both.

"Now," said Superintendent Pryde, "you are Don Francisco de Zayas y Tamago?"

He rapped off the elaborate name without hesitation and with a good Spanish accent.

Don Francisco looked at him.

"Is very difficult for me," he said.

"Yes, yes," said Superintendent Pryde, "I'm sure it is. And I'll do my best not to keep you a moment longer than is necessary."

He turned to Mrs. Craggs.

"Excuse me, madam," he said, "but I think I must claim priority for my business with Don Francisco."

He caught hold of the door and politely but firmly held it open for her.

"Certainly, sir," said Mrs. Craggs.

She made for the open door.

As she reached it Superintendent Pryde suddenly laid a hand on her shoulder.

"Wait a moment," he said, "you must be Mrs. Milhorne."

A tiny gleam of satisfaction came into his eyes as he accurately remembered the name.

But in a flash he saw from the expression on Mrs. Craggs's face that he had chosen wrongly.

"No," he said sharply, "my mistake. Mrs. Craggs, though, isn't it? Mrs. Emma Craggs, widow, 49 Harlaby Street, Flinwich, temporarily employed by the Flinwich Festival Company as a cleaner."

"That's right, sir," said Mrs. Craggs.

"And you were the lady who was first to the body, were you not?"

"I was as a matter of fact, sir."

Superintendent Pryde looked at her.

His eyes were large and surrounded by puckered lines of concentration. They gave the impression of churning into whatever was presented to their view.

"Yes," he said, "I shall be wanting a long talk with you later on. But tell me one thing first."

Mrs. Craggs looked steadily back.

"How was it that you told the doorkeeper here—Strutt, isn't it?—that it was a case of murder so quickly last night?"

"It was quite simple, sir," Mrs. Craggs replied. "I'd

heard the workings of the god's car being described like
when it was first put up, and I knew it couldn't come
down like by accident after the way it had gone all right
at the dress rehearsal not half an hour before. It wasn't
very likely that someone would take those weights off by
mistake, not with the warning notice so clear and everybody knowing about it."

" When was this description of the mechanics of the
contrivance given? "

The question was shot at Mrs. Craggs.

" As I said, sir, when it was first used. I happened to
be in the theatre and heard Don Francisco here tell
everybody how it worked. So that they'd know it was
safe, like."

" Everybody? Who was everybody? Can you tell me
exactly who was there? "

" That I can't, sir. There was so many of them. Most
of the cast of the opera, a good many stagehands, people
like Madame Glistanova and her husband, myself, my
friend, Mrs. Milhorne, any number of people."

Superintendent Pryde wasted no more time.

" Right," he said. " Thank you, Mrs. Craggs. As I
told you I shall want to see you again later. Does your
work keep you here? "

" Why, yes, sir, it does."

" Excellent. Then I shall be able to find you when I
want you."

He bowed Mrs. Craggs sharply out.

But before he had closed the door there came the sound
of half a dozen people running towards them.

Superintendent Pryde cocked his big head to one side.

" Aha," he said, " I think I know what we have here."

A moment later seven men came bursting round the corner.

" There he is," shouted the first of them.

" Ah," said the superintendent, " the gentlemen of the Press."

" Come on, now, Bill, what's in it? " one of the reporters asked quickly.

" Now, boys," the superintendent said, " I've only been in Flinwich three-quarters of an hour. Just time to hear what the men on the spot have to say. You can't expect anything yet."

" But is it murder? "

Superintendent Pryde flashed a quick look at Mrs. Craggs.

" Yes," he said, " it's murder all right. But I've got work to do."

He glanced at his watch.

" Lunch at one o'clock, gentlemen," he said. " I suppose you know which is the best pub? "

" Place called the Dog and Seaweed just round the corner," said one of the reporters instantly.

" I'll give you ten minutes there at one o'clock exactly," the superintendent said.

He closed the door of the office quietly but firmly, and left himself alone with Don Francisco and Detective-Sergeant Jenkins.

Mrs. Craggs went and got on with her work.

Occasionally as she swept and polished she caught sight of Superintendent Pryde going up to the flies or inspecting the god's car where it had been left on the stage. More often she saw his faithful shadow, Sergeant Jenkins, bringing one or other members of the company to Don Francisco's office, which its owner had now definitely lost. But Mrs. Craggs herself was not summoned there.

When it was nearly one o'clock she told Mrs. Milhorne, who had also not yet been questioned, that she was going home for dinner.

"Yes, but do you think we ought to?" Mrs. Milhorne said. "What would happen if they sent that Sergeant Jenkins to find us and we weren't there? He'd think one of us had done it. What would my old man say if a police car came and picked me up at home?"

"The super's going out for lunch at the Dog and Seaweed," Mrs. Craggs said. "I heard him tell those reporters so."

"Yes," said Mrs. Milhorne, "and that's another thing. Not one of that lot's so much as had a word with me yet. What if they couldn't find me when they wanted me? Of course, I don't agree with all their prying and questioning. But you've got to do what's right, that's what I say. And if you gets your picture in the paper next morning, well, there it is and you've got to lump it. It's the penalty for getting mixed up in a murder, and you've got to pay."

Mrs. Craggs examined her suffering expression.

"I wouldn't think they'd put you in the papers if you looked like that, dear," she said. "And I'm certainly not waiting about for reporters, that's one thing sure and certain."

She marched off towards the stage-door corridor.

Sitting on a discarded golden throne near the entrance to the corridor she saw Paul Pivoine. She stopped to have a word with him.

"Come on, now," she said, "there's no need to look

so down in the mouth quite. We've all got to bear it as best we may, you know."

Paul hardly looked up.

Mrs. Craggs took a step nearer and peered into his face in the dim backstage light.

"Why," she said, "I do believe you've taken it really badly. I'm sorry if I spoke out of turn, but I didn't think the poor girl meant more to you than she did to the rest of us."

Paul looked at her miserably.

"She did not mean anything to me," he said.

"Now what do you want to go saying that for?" asked Mrs. Craggs. "It's not true: anyone could see that."

"'She did not mean anything to me,' Paul repeated.

His large face set in a look of stubbornness.

"Well," said Mrs. Craggs, "I wasn't sure that she did before, but you can't tell me that you'd look so poorly as this if she wasn't no more than a passing acquaintance."

"What is it to you what she was?"

"There, there. It isn't anything to me and well you know it. The only thing is, if her being killed like this is going to make so much difference to you, that is something to me. I don't like to see a friend in trouble, and if a word of kindness will help they'll get it."

A look of mild cunning came into Paul's dull eyes.

"But, anyway," he said, "why shouldn't Mary being killed make me feel sad? She was someone I knew, some-one we all knew, and suddenly she was—— "

He balked at the word.

"And she was killed," he said in a rush. "She was killed and you tell me I am not to feel sad."

"Listen, my lad," said Mrs. Craggs, "I saw how you

were looking. I can still see it now, come to that. You're not just looking as if something a bit unpleasant had happened : you're looking as if the bottom had been knocked out of your world. I've seen people in trouble in my time, real trouble. And I know what they look like."

She regarded the big, ungainly pianist with sad eyes.

" It's a look there's no disguising," she said. " Because the people who have it are past disguising anything. So why not tell me the truth? Come on, ducks, it'll make you feel better, I promise you that."

" I cannot feel—— "

Paul broke off abruptly.

From down the corridor behind him had come first the noise of the stage-door banging closed and then a familiar sound.

A deep bass-baritone voice humming the refrain from the " Toreador's Song " in *Carmen*.

Contentedly and with immense cheerfulness.

" Him," said Paul.

His slouching form in the immense dusty gold throne became rigid.

" Yes," said Mrs. Craggs, " and listen to him. He knew Mary Arthur as well as you and listen to how he sounds. I dare say it's not in the best of taste to be so cheerful, but it's natural enough not to stay cast down for ever."

A moment later Jean-Artaban appeared at the end of the corridor just beside them.

He would have passed by without noticing them had not his son suddenly withdrawn to the depths of the gold throne in an effort to avoid being seen.

The abrupt movement just caught Jean-Artaban's eye.

He swung round.

" Ah," he said, " the good Madame Craggs. Good day to you, dear lady. And how is the worthy Monsieur Craggs? "

Mrs. Craggs pursed her lips.

" Gone," she said. " Gone this five years, and well you know it if you only stopped to think. You've asked me the same question a dozen times or more. And got the same answer."

Jean-Artaban was not abashed.

" Ah," he replied, " so the fascinating Madame Craggs is free. She is casting her eye about. If only I were not so faithful to my poor Alice Towell."

In the middle of this extravagant badinage his eye fell on his son.

" But I see my heir, who has so far escaped the thrall of a woman, is already entangled," he said.

Paul glowered.

" Yes," said Jean-Artaban, " his very silence confesses it."

He moved round and stood looking down at his son's ungainly body in the sombre magnificence of the painted throne.

Paul looked away.

" But what," said Jean-Artaban, " you do not greet your father? Come, a word."

Paul kept still as the fibreglass statue of a nymph from the Duke of Mantua's palace tucked into a corner just behind the throne.

" You," Jean-Artaban said. " You, my son. Greet your father. Speak. Say something. I insist."

Paul did not move.

Jean-Artaban laughed.

" Well," he said, " if it is possible, you are more spine-less than ever, my dear Paul. What has come over you? "

At this Paul did move. He shifted a little in the golden throne and looked up at Mrs. Craggs.

" I expect all this trouble's upsetting him, poor lad," she said. " It's enough to upset anyone."

She would have done better not to have responded to Paul's silent appeal.

Jean-Artaban turned to her.

" Trouble, my dear Madame Craggs? " he said. " What trouble is this? "

Mrs. Craggs looked him eye to eye.

" You know perfectly well what trouble it is," she said. " And if I may say so without speaking out of turn, you'd do well to pay a bit more attention to other people's feelings about it. Coming in here humming that tune like that."

" Ah," said Jean-Artaban.

He produced an expression of dawning enlightenment. It would have registered at the very back row of the gallery.

" Ah, now I begin to understand. It is this silly girl's death, and you think that we should all go about in deep mourning. And this stupid boy, I suppose he was in love with her."

Paul leapt up.

" And you," he shouted. " What about you? What were your relations with her? Perhaps it is easy to see why you sing so happily? Perhaps you think that if you look content nobody will believe that you really are content, content because you have succeeded in doing what you wished to do? Content because you have killed Mary? "

CHAPTER XIII

" WELL NOW, that's a very pretty accusation."

All three of them looked round.

Standing a few feet away with an expression of amused interest curling his jutting black eyebrows was Superintendent Pryde.

He grinned sharply when he saw the effect his sudden interruption had had. Paul looked as if he was wishing that the golden throne would split open and let him fall to some deep, unapproachable recess under the stage. Jean-Artaban looked plainly and single-mindedly furious that he had been so utterly deprived of the initiative. Mrs. Craggs looked annoyed that she had been taken advantage of in some way.

" Yes," said Superintendent Pryde, " a very pretty accusation. But not a very pretty thing to accuse anybody of, especially one's own father."

Jean-Artaban looked yet more furious. He preferred to effect his introductions himself. To find a policeman knowing both himself and his son was not at all to his liking.

But he was not going to be allowed to put things right.

Superintendent Pryde stepped sharply forward and stood between father and son. He looked down at the ungainly pianist who had slumped back awkwardly on the throne.

" Suppose you tell me just what was at the back of it all," he said.

An order given.

Paul shifted uneasily on the broad surface of the great golden chair.

" There is nothing at the back of it," he muttered.

" Come, lad, that won't do. You have just made a very serious accusation. You can't do that without having some reason. I am the police officer investigating this case : you will tell me what you meant by your statement."

Paul glowered.

" I meant that he killed her."

" You meant that your father killed Miss Arthur. Yes, we all understand that perfectly well. Now, will you please tell us exactly what led to this accusation. Why do you think he murdered her? "

Silence.

" Come on, lad, speak up. Why do you think he murdered her? "

" I said why," Paul muttered.

" Oh, you did, did you? Then perhaps you'll just repeat it."

Paul looked up a little.

" Why should I? " he said. " You heard me."

" You'll repeat what you said."

A moment of challenge. An instant of suspense.

But there could be no doubt of the outcome. Characters a great deal stronger than Paul Pivoine would not have stood up to the tone of total conviction the superintendent brought to the struggle. He beyond question meant to get his answer.

He got it.

" It is because he comes here making such an impression of not caring," Paul said. " I know him. It is the sort of thing he delights in. If he killed Mary, he would take care to behave like a triumphant murderer."

" If he killed her."

The superintendent pounced.

" If he killed her. It's come to that now, has it? A moment ago it was ' You killed Mary.' Now we seem to be hearing a different story."

Paul gripped the two wide arms of the wooden throne and started slightly out of his seat.

" But he was there," he said loudly. " He was the one who was there. In the best place. Looking down from above on everybody. He could see whether he was being watched. He could choose his moment."

Each jet of accusation delivered on a louder and louder note.

Superintendent Pryde spoke more quietly than usual.

" I see, lad," he said. " And what else? "

" What else? What else? Isn't that enough? "

" No, lad, it's not enough. It's nothing like enough. What more is there? "

Silence.

But this time the superintendent did not demand his answer. He left the silence to grow.

Nobody said anything.

The superintendent stood looking steadily down at Paul. Jean-Artaban towered behind him but was so completely ignored that even he did nothing to break the spell. Mrs. Craggs knew better than to speak, but her worn eyes went from one to another of the group. And hunched on the gilt throne Paul could be seen writhing under the tension.

At last he spoke.

" It is all."

Superintendent Pryde turned sharply on his heel.

" And you waste my time with that? "

The words spat out.

For half an instant Paul looked as if he was going to reply. He had not offered to waste the superintendent's time. But almost at once he plainly realised that in this sort of encounter might is right. He turned and looked at the white-washed brick wall beside him.

" Well, my dear sir," said Jean-Artaban, " I am glad to hear you are not the sort of man to be taken in easily with such poppycock."

The superintendent glanced up at him from under his formidable jutting eyebrows.

" No," he said, " I'm not."

He turned towards the stage-door corridor.

" I find you already know me," Jean-Artaban said. " And I confess I am not altogether surprised. But you have me at a disadvantage."

" Oh, really? " said the superintendent.

He did not stop to deliver this reply.

Jean-Artaban set off with him along the corridor.

" We have not been introduced, you know," he said.

" No," said the superintendent.

He took half a dozen quick paces.

" I shall be seeing you in due course, sir," he said. " I'll state my name and business then. And now if you'll excuse me I have an important conference."

He glanced as he spoke at the big clock hanging from the back wall of the stage doorkeeper's cubbyhole. Its elaborate hands were pointing exactly to one o'clock on the ornate Roman numerals.

The superintendent hurried out.

At his heels went the anonymous figure of Sergeant Jenkins.

Jean-Artaban looked at them.

A heavy purple flush came up in a dense line just under his eyes.

::   ::

After dinner Mrs. Craggs clocked back on.

Mr. Strutt wrote the time against her name in his ledger.

" Though why anyone should be paid for hanging about watching the murder squad at their antics is more than I can say," he remarked.

Mrs. Craggs drew herself up.

" I hope you're not meaning that my work isn't getting done," she said. " Because if so let me tell you that I've done just as much to-day as I do on any other day."

Mr. Strutt looked up.

" Well," he said, " there's some who aren't back from their dinners yet."

He pointed a heavy, arthritic finger at Mrs. Mil-horne's name in his ledger. There was no entry in the time column.

" I can't help what others do," said Mrs. Craggs. " That's none of my business. But for myself I can speak, and I'd like to point out that I didn't leave till gone one and I'm back exactly on two."

" I never said you weren't," said Mr. Strutt. " I hope I know when anybody comes in or out of that door, never mind whether I have to enter them in the book or not."

He drew the arthritic finger down the side of his bulbous, blood-bursting nose.

" It's a good thing I have got eyes in my head, too," he said. " Otherwise I don't know where Mr. Superintendent Pryde of the Yard would be, for all his cleverness."

" Pryde of the Yard," said Mrs. Craggs.

A sharp dose of scorn.

Mr. Strutt shrugged his still square shoulders, relic of a distant military past.

" It's what the papers call him," he said.

" The papers."

Mr. Strutt looked up at her.

" That reminds me," he said. " One of them reporters was asking me this morning how I'd first come to hear about the murder."

He looked down in the direction of the ledger, smiling a little under the bristles of his moustache.

" 'Course," he added, " I took good care not to bring your name into it, Mrs. Craggs. I know you wouldn't want to go getting mixed up with the Press and finding yourself talked about."

" And as a matter of fact I wouldn't," Mrs. Craggs said. " Though I dare say you thought otherwise, for all your consideration of my feelings."

" I thought of no such thing."

Mr. Strutt's moustache bristled more vigorously than ever.

" I knew you wouldn't have the strength of mind to face up to it, my dear," he said. " It takes a bit of backbone to know you're being looked at wherever you go and not to care a button about it. I know. I was used to it in the Army. A regimental sergeant major is a figure in an army town. You take my word for it."

" So I've heard you remark before."

" So it won't come as no shock to me to-morrow morning to find myself a sort of hero."

" Oh, yes."

" Oh, yes, indeed. I was able to give the principal
national newspapers a very clear account of just exactly
what happened last night in this building."

" Told them who killed the poor little thing, I
suppose? "

" I did not. I should hope I know my place better than
that. But I was able to tell them the next best thing. I
was able to tell them, and the police, just exactly who was
in the building at the time of the incident."

" Which incident would that be, Mr. Strutt? "

" The incident of the death of Mary Arthur. Yes, I
think they'll be very glad that I happened to be in this
box last night."

" Because you could give them some idea of who came
in and out like? "

" Some idea. Some idea, indeed. Listen to me, my
good woman, I told the super exactly who was left in the
theatre after the rehearsal and who had gone out. Down
to the last member of the orchestra. That's the value of
system. You stick to your system and you know just
what's happening."

" I see. And the superintendent took your word for
it? "

Mr. Strutt's already red face went contortedly purple.

" I hope as how you're not doubting me, Mrs. Craggs? "

" I didn't say I was, did I, Mr. Strutt? I was more
interested in the police methods."

Mr. Strutt sat up more straightly.

" If you was to be less interested in police methods and

more interested in cleaning methods perhaps we might be getting somewhere," he said.

"Certainly, we might. If you don't want to pass the time of day, I'm sure I'm quite ready to be getting on. I don't go till I've finished, so the sooner I start the sooner I get away home."

"Very well then," Mr. Strutt said as Mrs. Craggs turned to leave the cubbyhole, "then I may as well set your mind at rest by informing you that the super indulged in a very thorough check-up on my methods as a result of which he declared himself thoroughly satisfied."

"I'm sure I'm very glad to hear it. But I can't help wondering how you can be so sure nobody came in through the foyer all the same."

"I thought you might be wondering that," said Mr. Strutt.

His eyes gleamed and glittered with triumph.

"And the answer's perfectly simple, my dear. Before I came on duty I happened to make a personal inspection of the entire building and I concentrated especially on making sure all doors other than the stage door, over which I have personal supervision, were securely locked and fastened. A fact which the local police themselves collaborated last night."

"I'm sure that must have been very consoling for you."

But Mr. Strutt intended to wallow in his triumph for longer than this. He ignored the note of finality which Mrs. Craggs had brought to her remark. He ignored it totally.

"So," he said, " I was able to provide Pryde of the Yard with exactly what he was looking for, if you ask me.

I was able to provide him from my own knowledge with a list."

" That'd be a list of who was in the theatre when Miss Arthur was killed. I hope you remembered to include me in on it? "

" You were in the theatre : you were on the list."

Mr. Strutt contemplated the silver buttons running down the front of his uniform.

Mrs. Craggs made another move towards the door.

" I shall just give you the names without comment," Mr. Strutt said. " I don't think it's my place to comment."

" I should be very interested to hear," Mrs. Craggs said.

She was going to hear and would put the best face she could on it.

" Very well then," Mr. Strutt said. " There's eleven names to be mentioned."

He held up ten fingers, stubby and swollen at the joints.

" One," he said, " Don Francisco Whatdoyoucallhim, the director. Two : Mr. Pivoine senior. Three : Mrs. Pivoine. Four : Mr. Franz Prahler, the singer. Five : Madame Glistanova. Six : her husband. Seven : Miss Clarone. Eight : Mr. Pivoine junior. Nine : young Albert Sime, left on the brakes, poor lad. Ten : Mrs. Milhorne."

The ten stubby fingers had all gone down now. Mr. Strutt popped one of them up again.

" And eleven," he said, " Mrs. Emma Craggs."

Mrs. Craggs nodded.

" And that was everybody? " she said.

" Of course it was everybody. I checked them, didn't I? "

Mrs. Craggs sighed.

" Well," she said, " I wouldn't like to be in your shoes, Mr. Strutt, honest I wouldn't."

" And why not? "

" To think of the responsibility."

" What responsibility? "

Mr. Strutt glared.

" It's only your word that the eleven of us are going to be made into suspects by the murder squad, on your word alone."

Mr. Strutt shook his head sadly from side to side.

" Ah, well, Mrs. Craggs, I can't help that, now can I? If the eleven of you were the only ones in the theatre at the time, then the murder squad is bound to suspect you, isn't it? And if I know that you were the only ones, well then, I've got to say it, haven't I? However much weight the responsibility is."

He looked grave.

" But supposing you might have made a mistake, Mr. Strutt? " said Mrs. Craggs.

Mr. Strutt shook his head. Briefly.

" Ah," he said, " it's not a position I would wish on you, Mrs. Craggs. It's not a position I would wish on any woman. But a man, a man who is used to taking responsibility, now that's different."

He leant forward across the narrow table on which the ledger rested.

" You know," he said, " it makes no difference to me, not one bit. I know who the eleven in the theatre at the time of the crime were, and I tell the police. It's automatic."

He leant back again till the top of his chair fitted comfortably into the small of his back.

" I don't feel the weight of a thing like that one single bit."

Mrs. Craggs shook her head.

" And it's all on you," she said.

" All on me."

" Your unsupported word."

Mr. Strutt sat up a little.

The back edge of the chair was no longer in contact with his body.

" You're not suggesting nothing, I should hope," he said.

" You're not having doubts, Mr. Strutt? "

" Doubts? Doubts? What do you mean, doubts? How could I have doubts? I told the super, I told the Press. I couldn't have doubts about a thing like that now. How do you—— "

Mr. Strutt suddenly leapt to his feet.

He peered round past Mrs. Craggs.

" How do you do, sir? How do you do, Superintendent? " he said.

Superintendent Pryde came in at the door of the cubbyhole.

" Good afternoon, Mr. Strutt," he said. " Did I hear you telling this good lady about how you were able to help us this morning? "

" You did, sir."

Mr. Strutt sent a reproving glance out towards Mrs. Craggs. He bestowed it.

" Yes," said the superintendent, " you gave us information of great value, Mr. Strutt. I'm very grateful to your sharp eyes and retentive memory. The lads of the 14th Yeomanry may not have blessed them, but I do."

He shot a quick look at Mr. Strutt to see how his remembering of the particular regiment had gone down.

It had been a decided success.

" Ah ha, sir," said Mr. Strutt, " I see I'm not the only one to have a retentive memory. Why, I suppose I must have mentioned the name of the regiment I had the honour to serve in anything up to a hundred times to Mrs. Craggs here. But do you think she could tell—— "

He interrupted himself to throw a quick salute in the direction of the door.

" Afternoon, Mr. Prahler, sir," he called.

" There you are," said the superintendent. " How about that, Jenkins, for keen observation? "

" Not bad, sir," Jenkins replied.

He kept the three syllables to a minimum of anonymity.

Franz Prahler, who had indeed slipped very unobtrusively into the theatre, now turned and came back on hearing his name called.

" Good afternoon, Strutt," he said. " I'm sorry I didn't drop in for a chat. I—I was rather preoccupied. I'm glad you called out."

He hopped up on to the edge of Mr. Strutt's table and sat comfortably swinging his legs. Mr. Strutt looked at him with tolerant disapproval. No one else would have dared to sit on his table, but equally no one else would have addressed him in the same unselfconsciously friendly way.

" Well, Herr Prahler," said the superintendent, " I

L

shall have to have a chat with you a little later on to-day,
I'm sorry to say. Duty's duty, though I'd much rather
listen to you sing than listen to your answers to my
questions. I haven't had the luck to hear you in real life
since your concert at the Festival Hall in—let me see—
April two years back. Yes, April the eighteenth, if I
remember rightly. A wonderful occasion."

Franz looked delighted.

" Little did I think Detective-Superintendent Pryde
was listening that night," he said. " Pryde of the Yard.
I should have been frightened, I can tell you."

The superintendent laughed.

" I think it would take a bit more than me to frighten
you off your note, Herr Prahler," he said.

Franz wagged his finger.

" Ah," he said, " frightened I would have been, yes.
But frightened so that I sang badly, no. I tell you,
liebling, every time before I go on the stage or on the
concert platform I am still sweating like a pig with fright.
But always when I start to sing the first note, poof, away
goes my fright. It is always the same."

He caught one knee in his clasped hands and leant back
contentedly reviewing the mystery of his voice's effect.
But suddenly the look of glowing pleasure vanished.

He swung forward off the table.

" But now I must go," he said. " I am really in such a
hurry. I just came to collect a score I left in my dressing-
room. Superintendent, if you want me, you will find me
at my hotel, the Flinwich Arms. It is a very top room
because of not disturbing the other guests with practising."

He shot away with such speed that no one had time to
comment.

His abrupt departure sent the others off as well. Superintendent Pryde and Sergeant Jenkins went to Don
Francisco's office to continue their series of interviews and
Mrs. Craggs made for the gentlemen's side dressing-
rooms with broom, dustpan and brush.

As she reached the foot of the iron stairs Jean-Artaban
appeared suddenly out of the shadows above her. He
seemed as startled to see her as she had been by him.

It was only when he was two or three yards past her
that he turned and spoke to her.

" Ah," he said, " the *si belle* Madame Craggs. How I
envy that excellent Monsieur Craggs."

Mrs. Craggs looked at him squarely under her square
hat.

" Gone," she said. " He's gone. Don't you remember
nothing? "

But Jean-Artaban had not waited to listen.

Mrs. Craggs climbed the stairs and started on her tasks.
She worked steadily and without further disturbance.
The cancellation of that night's performance, coupled
with the superintendent's activities, gave her for once an
uninterrupted spell of work.

But it was a good hour later before she reached Franz
Prahler's room, so it was with considerable surprise
that she found her perfunctory knock on the door was
answered.

" Yes, yes," the golden-voiced tenor called out, " who
is there? "

He sounded rather frightened.

" It's only me, Herr Prahler, come to give the room a
bit of a clean-up," Mrs. Craggs called back.

The door opened.

" Oh," said Franz, " it's you."

" I could come back later if you liked," said Mrs. Craggs. " Only as you mentioned you were going to your hotel I thought the room would be vacant like."

" No, no," said Franz, looking at her with unusual intensity, " come in. Please come in and start your work. I am just going. And in any case you will not disturb me."

Mrs. Craggs made no comment on these two contradictory statements. She came into the smallish room, laid down her dustpan and brush and began sweeping.

Franz sat down in the single small modern arm-chair. There was no sign of the score he had spoken about coming to fetch.

Mrs. Craggs methodically swept away.

" Well, *liebling*," said Franz, " this is a terrible day." Mrs. Craggs sighed.

" It's certainly sad, sir," she said. " As sad as could be, a pretty little thing like that going in the prime of life, as you might say."

" And such a voice, *liebling*, such a voice."

Franz spoke on a note of hushed reverence. A sacred thing was being discussed.

" Poor kid," said Mrs. Craggs. " You knew her better than most, didn't you, sir? Can you tell me if she had any particular friends over here? I know she was an orphan back in Australia."

Franz perked up.

" Ah," he said, " I know what you mean. Whenever a woman talks about ' particular friends ' she means lovers, yes? "

Mrs. Craggs finished her sweeping, leant her broom in

a corner and began methodically moving the assorted objects from one side of the dressing-table in front of the big flat mirror with its edging of naked electric-light bulbs. She said nothing.

In a moment Franz went on.

" Well, no," he said, " I can tell you. She did not have many friends of any sort here. She was a worker that one. You wouldn't believe it perhaps, but she had a will of iron in her little body so weak."

He sat in the aseptic arm-chair looking down at the floor.

" She worked so well," he said, " and it is all now for nothing."

" Yes," Mrs. Craggs agreed, " it does seem rather a waste in some ways, doesn't it? "

" A waste. A waste. It is a tragedy. So many years of work I had done with her. I had taken this tuneless, untamed voice from the outback of Australia and I had made it into a thing of beauty, a delicate but unbreakable thing. It would have started a new life for me and it is gone."

He looked over at Mrs. Craggs. There were tears in his eyes.

" It is gone my chance," he said. " And what will happen to me when my voice goes? "

" Well," said Mrs. Craggs briskly, " that isn't going to be for a good many years yet, is it? "

Franz shot her a quick look.

" No, no," he said. " Of course not. Not for a long time. But all the same one day it is certain to go. And if I then cannot take pupils, what will happen to me? "

He stared at the ceiling.

" Why has this been done to me? " he said.

Mrs. Craggs went to the little window, opened it with a jerk and shook her duster vigorously into the chilly autumn air.

" It's what's been done to her that worries me," she said.

Perhaps because her face had been turned to the open window as she had spoken Franz had not heard. Or perhaps he chose to ignore such an unsympathetic view. In any case he made no immediate reply, and when he did speak again it was to follow his own previous train of thought.

" This is what I cannot understand, Mrs. Craggs," he said, " it is as I have told you : she had really no friends, no one who knew her more than a little. So why was she killed? There is no reason, no reason at all."

He bounced out of the aseptic arm-chair and paced quickly up and down the little room.

" I tell you," he said, " I have thought a lot about this since it happened. I have thought of little else. And there is no reason why she should have been killed, absolutely no reason whatever. So why was she? Why? Why? Why? "

Mrs. Craggs stood watching him without moving. The expression on her time-worn face under the squat, square hat was harshly serious.

" Suppose they didn't want to kill her at all," she said.

CHAPTER XIV

IT WAS NOT the answer Franz Prahler had expected.

He stopped his rapid, hopping prowl and stood for an instant looking at Mrs. Craggs.

" What do you mean ' They didn't want to kill her '? " he asked. " I am afraid it is no good trying to convince anybody that it was an accident. Oh, no, no, no, my good lady, that is impossible. Everybody is agreed on that."

He turned and started striding up and down the little room again.

" No, *liebling*," he said, " it shows your good heart not to wish to think anybody is a murderer, but it is not practical. It is not practical at all."

Mrs. Craggs began moving the objects on the dressing-table back on to the half she had dusted and polished.

" That's not what I—— "

A sharp tap on the door interrupted her.

Franz stopped his quick pacing and looked at the door.

" Yes? What is it? " he called out.

" It's me, sir, Sergeant Jenkins. I was looking for one of the cleaning-ladies, a Mrs. Craggs. The superintendent would like a word with her. I thought I heard her in with you."

" But come in, come in," Franz said. " Yes, Mrs. Craggs is here. We were just chatting as she worked. Now I must be on my way."

Without picking up a score or anything else he hopped

out past the nondescript Sergeant Jenkins and clattered
down the iron stairs. Mrs. Craggs put her duster into the
apron pocket and wiped her hands.

" I'm ready," she said. " He's in the director's office,
isn't he? "

The sergeant led the way.

Superintendent Pryde had succeeded in transforming
Don Francisco's office. It was not clear to Mrs. Craggs at
first exactly what he had done. But the office no longer
looked like the showplace of an advanced airline. It had a
more homely, more squalid look.

The big abstract canvases still hung from the walls but
next to the most striking of them, Mrs. Craggs realised,
the superintendent had hung from a fitting at the top of
the window his well-used mackintosh. And on the smart
ebony desk he had planked down a battered brief-case, a
plate of sandwiches and two bottles of beer.

Mrs. Craggs looked at the food and drink sternly.

The superintendent appeared to guess what she was
thinking.

" I'm sorry I've made such a mess," he said. " Perhaps
in fact you'd be kind enough to deal with it when we've
had our little talk."

He smiled broadly.

" The fact of the matter is," he said, " that I didn't get
any lunch. I had a meeting and it lasted longer than I
expected. So I got hold of a little light refreshment afterwards."

" Very natural, I'm sure."

The superintendent looked at her.

" Well, now," he said, " let's get down to business for
the present. Would you be good enough to take a seat? "

He gestured towards the elegant Swedish chair which he had set facing the desk at an uncompromising right angle.

Mrs. Craggs sat on the edge of it.

The superintendent opened a buff file in front of him and began slowly reading the single slip of paper it contained.

Mrs. Craggs was not going to put up with this.

" I hear from Mr. Strutt that you're satisfied there were only eleven of us in the whole building at the time of the murder," she said.

Superintendent Pryde looked up sharply.

" Well," he said, " I can see I shan't have to beat about the bush with you, Mrs. Craggs. Yes, subject to further inquiries, you can take it that there were eleven people only here at the time in question. I wonder if you can tell me their names? "

" Of course I can. You don't think I wouldn't have worked it out for myself, do you? There was the three Pivoines, the four if you count la Clarone, the two Einfalts, Herr Prahler and Don Francisco, young Albert Sime on the brakes and Mrs. Milhorne and myself."

" That seems to be correct."

" So you shouldn't have much difficulty, should you? "

Superintendent Pryde shifted in his chair.

" Let me tell you," he said, " that that's by no means the case. It isn't often you have a murder committed and find eleven people each of whom could have done it without being seen by any of the others."

The look of surprise on Mrs. Craggs's face seemed to please him. He relaxed in his chair again.

" Yes," he went on, " unless you're going to tell me that you were able to see any of the eleven without them seeing you, that is precisely the situation that confronts me."

He sounded as if he was some gourmet facing a large, rare and appetising dish.

He tilted his chair back.

" It's quite extraordinary really," he said. " You get a comparatively small area such as the stage of this theatre, and you have eleven people there. But it so happens that at a certain point in time, i.e., at the instant the weights were taken off that god's car contrivance, not one of those eleven people was with another of them."

" Not Mr. Einfalt with Madame Glistanova? " asked Mrs. Craggs.

The superintendent's two jutting black eyebrows came crashing together.

" I see you keep your eyes open, Mrs. Craggs," he said. " Yes, one would have expected that gentleman to be dancing attendance. But it so happens that he was not. Even the most devoted of husbands, it seems, are at the mercy of calls of nature."

He grinned tigerishly.

" The nearest gentlemen's lavatory is off the stage-door corridor," he said.

" There's something you could tell me about that," said Mrs. Craggs.

The superintendent looked a little astonished.

" Is it clean and all that? " Mrs. Craggs said. " Is it properly looked after? It's had to be left in that Mr Strutt's charge, and I don't know what sort of a state it may have got into. I dare say he thinks he's above that sort of job. Sergeant-major and all."

Superintendent Pryde looked uneasy.

" Jenkins," he said, " did you notice whether the place was clean? "

" Might have been better, sir," said Sergeant Jenkins non-committally.

" Well, there you are then," said the superintendent, " independent evidence."

He coughed.

" As I was saying, Mr. Einfalt was where we mentioned. He left his wife sitting in that golden chair thing which was standing just where it was this morning, round the corner from the corridor out of most people's sight. Then, of course, Monsieur Pivoine was, as his son pointed out, up in the top of the flies alone. His wife was waiting for him alone in his dressing-room. Herr Prahler was in his dressing-room, also alone. Signorina Clarone was on the other side of the theatre in her dressing-room. Mrs. Milhorne was in Miss Glass's room sweeping it out. Young Sime was standing over his brakes in the fly gallery. Don Francisco was sitting in the stalls by himself, and the same applies to young Monsieur Pivoine in the orchestra pit, though he was at least at the piano which does account for him."

He suddenly swung forward over the plate with its solitary uneaten sandwich.

" And that leaves you," he said.

" And as you have probably heard by now I was in the dressing-room next to Mrs. Milhorne also on my own," said Mrs. Craggs.

With composure.

" Yes," said the superintendent. " So you told my colleague in the county force last night."

Mrs. Craggs said nothing.

" You've no proof you were where you say you were? "

" If I had to have proof every time I went to do out a room I'd never be at the end of it."

" Well, that's as may be. But as it is we've only got your unsupported word for the fact that you remained alone in that dressing-room till you heard the god's car crash."

" That's right."

Silence.

The superintendent turned over the piece of paper in the buff file in front of him. The back was perfectly blank.

Mrs. Craggs, sitting on the edge of the upright Swedish chair squarely facing the desk, looked at the paper.

Superintendent Pryde turned it over again.

" You realise," he said, " that if you had left that dressing-room and run quietly down the iron stairs you could have got to where the weights were without anybody seeing you? "

" But as I didn't leave the dressing-room nobody could have seen me anyway," Mrs. Craggs said.

The superintendent leaned forward patiently.

" Let me explain," he said. " The ropes holding the god's car, as they call it, hang down through the fly gallery at the back of the theatre. On the end of them hang, or hung, the weights. When the car was fully up the weights would be at stage level in the dark under the fly gallery."

" Where I saw them during the dress rehearsal," Mrs. Craggs put in helpfully.

The superintendent's black eyebrows swooped towards each other.

"You saw the weights during the dress rehearsal?"

"Yes, sir."

"At what time was this?"

"Just after the car had gone back up."

"I see. And tell me: was the warning notice still on them?"

He rummaged in one of the files piled untidily on the elegant ebony desk.

After a moment he fished out a piece of white cardboard with the words, "Danger Do Not Remove These Weights" painted on it in red ink.

"This," he said. "Was it in its right place when you saw the weights at the end of the dress rehearsal?"

"Let me think a minute," said Mrs. Craggs.

She closed her eyes.

"Yes," she said. "Yes, it was there all right. I can see it just as it was."

"You didn't mention this to my county colleague," Superintendent Pryde said.

"No. Well, it never came into my mind like. And he didn't ask me anything about it."

The superintendent sighed and shot a quick look at Sergeant Jenkins.

"Well," he said, "the fact has emerged now at least. The notice was in position just about the end of the rehearsal. Right?"

"That's right, sir."

"Good."

The superintendent leant back.

"So now," he said, "I was just explaining to you the exact set-up round the place where the weights were."

He looked into the air above Mrs. Craggs. His eyes were puckered in concentration.

"The weights came right under the fly gallery where it was even darker than the rest of the backstage area," he said. "And as it so happened, on each side of them there was a fairly large object which would give excellent cover to anyone approaching the place along the back wall of the theatre right under the gallery. On the right as you face the wall there was what they call a thundersheet, a big sheet of metal hanging in a frame which makes a noise like thunder when you hit it. And on the left there was——"

His concentration beamed into the air.

"On the left there was a mock fig-tree in a tub. Fig-leaves are pretty large, as you may know. You could hide quite effectively behind them."

"Yes, I know it was there, and the thundersheet," Mrs. Craggs said. "Monsieur Pivoine pretended to knock into it once when someone else was singing. It does make a noise like thunder all right, sort of hollow."

"Yes," said the superintendent. "So you knew the lay-out all right. And you realise what it means? Anyone, someone, could have got to the weights with very little chance of being seen."

"What about Monsieur Pivoine spotting them from above?" said Mrs. Craggs.

"Yes, you're quite right. He was the most likely person to see what went on. Only he was peering forwards on to the stage watching for his cue, and not looking backwards into the area behind the set. And as for young Sime, who was also in a good position to see anybody, well,

I don't think I've ever had the pleasure of dealing with a less useful witness."

The superintendent glanced up at Sergeant Jenkins for confirmation. The sergeant was prompt to nod agreement.

"Not only did the stupid lad faint as soon as he saw the ropes flying through the brake blocks," Superintendent Pryde said, "but he spent the whole time he was up in the gallery staring at the levers to make sure he would release the right ones when the time came."

"They ought never to have left him there all by himself," said Mrs. Craggs. "He's only a boy."

"Well, that's as may be, but the fact remains that he was completely unhelpful to me. Any one of ten people— eleven if you count Sime himself—could have got at those weights."

He looked straight at Mrs. Craggs.

"You could have done," he said.

Mrs. Craggs said nothing.

The superintendent turned over the piece of paper in the open buff file. And suddenly remembered its blank back.

"Look, Mrs. Craggs," he said, "I've already had occasion to remark that you appear to be a woman of keen observation. You notice things."

He paused and looked up into the air above her head.

"I suppose it comes from your job," he said. "If your duty is to clear up any messes that are made, then you keep an eye out for things."

He leant forward and looked at her directly.

"However," he said, "that is by the way. The point is : have you seen or heard anything in the past few days, either before the murder or after it, that you think might have a bearing on the matter."

" I can't say that I have."

" No? Well, I didn't expect you to be able to answer yes. After all, you haven't got a mind trained to know what might or might not be relevant to an affair like this. So I want to put a different question to you."

The large eyes boring into her.

" I want to put this question : have you at any time in the recent past noticed anything unusual, anything at all, about any of the ten other people in the theatre when this business happened? "

Mrs. Craggs did not answer immediately.

" No," she replied at last. " No, I can't say I have."

" Nothing whatsoever? "

" Nothing."

" Nothing, no matter how trivial or silly? "

" I said nothing."

The superintendent leant back in his chair.

" Well," he said, " let's go about it another way."

He picked up a pencil and twiddled it.

" For instance," he said, " when Sergeant Jenkins here asked you to come and see me, what were you doing? Where were you at that very moment? "

" I was working. I was in Herr Prahler's dressing-room."

" I see. Now, did you notice anything out of the ordinary there? Anything at all not quite as you're used to seeing it? "

" Are you suggesting that I go prying round when I'm at work in the dressing-rooms ? "

The superintendent smiled.

" No, no. Not one bit. Though, mind you, I wouldn't blame you if you did. What's the harm in it? What's the harm in a little natural curiosity? "

" Plenty, if the person you're being curious about happens to be in the room at the time."

" Oh. Oh, I see. Herr Prahler was there, was he? "

" He was."

" And you talked to him? "

" He talked to me."

" What about? "

" What do you think? He talked about the murder, of course. When a thing like that happens you stop talking about the weather. You've something worth discussing at last. And in any case it's worrying him. That girl meant a lot to him as a pupil. For his future, like."

" Very good. He said that, did he? "

" More or less."

" Excellent. And what else did he say? As far as you're able to remember, of course."

" He didn't say all that much. Only that the poor girl was a hard worker and didn't have many friends over here."

" That we already know."

" You asked me what he said and I'm telling you."

" Quite right, quite right. You just go on telling me. Don't let what you think might or might not be important make any difference. You just tell me everything."

" All right. Well, he said it was a terrible pity her being killed because now no one would ever know what a good teacher he was. He thought it'd be too late or something. Then he went on to wonder why anyone should kill her at all."

M

" I don't blame him. So do I. And what then? "

" Nothing."

" Nothing? "

" Yes, I was just making some sort of remark like in answer and your Sergeant Jenkins knocked at the door."

" I see."

Superintendent Pryde tapped six or seven times with the butt end of the pencil on the surface of the ebony desk.

He sighed.

" What were you saying to him? "

" Just that it looked to me as if the girl wasn't meant to be killed at all."

The black jutting eyebrows shot together.

" That it was really meant to be Monsieur Pivoine, you know," Mrs. Craggs explained.

" I see."

Superintendent Pryde stood up.

" Well," he said, " I think that will be all."

Mrs. Craggs got up and took the dirty dishes off the desk.

" By the way," the superintendent said, " I wouldn't go mentioning that notion of yours to too many people. Might get you into trouble, you know. It's not very likely really."

" I never said it was," Mrs. Craggs replied. " I only told you what I said to Herr Prahler. You asked me, you know. We were just going over what happened, the way people do. It was my turn to say something, and so that's what I said."

The superintendent nodded.

" Oh, yes," he said. " There's no reason why you shouldn't have made the remark. But I thought I ought to draw your attention to the fact that it's the sort of thing that makes for bad feeling. It would make people think a whole lot of people had got reasons for being a murderer. I dare say you hadn't thought of that aspect. Good day."

He held open the door for Mrs. Craggs and her load of dishes.

In the corridor outside Mrs. Craggs saw Mrs. Milhorne.

" Hallo, dear," she said, " I missed you when I came back dinner time."

" Yes," said Mrs. Milhorne, " I came all over queer when I was having dinner and I had to have a bit of a lay-down before I came back."

" You all right now, dear? "

" Yes, thank you, dear. Not too bad, that is. Of course, it all started up again the moment I arrived. I still feel fluttery when I think of it."

" What of? "

" Of it. Of that Pryde of the Yard."

" Oh. You been to see him, too, have you, dear? "

" Yes. No sooner was I back when he sent for me. That's why I was waiting for you when you came out. I thought you might be feeling like me."

" I'm feeling all right," said Mrs. Craggs.

" Well, I dare say you didn't have the time of it I did. And then I've got what I call a sensitive nature."

" So I've heard you say."

" So you can't wonder that it made me feel not too good, can you? "

" I don't see why it should have done. He couldn't eat you."

" No, but it was the strain. You didn't have that.

That's what makes the difference. Especially to someone like me."

" What strain? "

" The strain of not telling, of course."

" Not telling? What have you got not to tell, I should like to know."

" What I heard. I couldn't tell him that, could I? I couldn't tell him all that."

CHAPTER XV

MRS. CRAGGS looked at Mrs. Milhorne. Unbendingly.

" When I was in there just now," she said, " he asked me whether I had heard or seen anything that might have a bearing on this business. Did he ask you the same? "

" Oh, yes," said Mrs. Milhorne. " That was the worst moment really. I thought I should faint."

" And you didn't tell him about whatever it is you heard? "

Mrs. Milhorne bridled.

" Of course I didn't," she said. " I keep telling you, don't I? It was all I could do not to show it on my face. That's the trouble with feeling things so deep : they show."

" And all this has definitely got something to do with Mary Arthur? "

" Of course it has. It was her, don't you realise that? It was her I couldn't help overhearing. That was what made it so dreadful."

" And what exactly did you listen to her saying? And who was she saying it to? "

Mrs. Craggs did not attempt to conceal her curiosity.

" But to Jean-Artaban."

A certain delicacy of feeling forbade Mrs. Milhorne adding " Who else could it be? "

" So you heard Jean-Artaban and Mary Arthur saying something? Something that showed there was something between them, or what? "

" It wasn't Jean-Artaban I heard so much. It was her. Though I could see he was there. They were standing just inside the scene dock. I suppose to get a bit of privacy. But, of course, there's no door there, though it is out of the way. So if anyone was near enough they could hear everything that was being said."

" It was Mary Arthur who was doing the speaking, was it? "

" It certainly was. And using language, too. I didn't never think a lady would use language quite like that."

" Mary Arthur was a nice kid, but she was no lady."

" Well," said Mrs. Milhorne, " perhaps it was her being Australian. Because you can't tell me she wasn't a lady, underneath. She was a singer."

" You're a singer because you've got a voice. It doesn't make any difference to the sort of person you are."

" Well, I don't believe that."

" It's just a matter of having been born with vocal chords a tiny bit different from everyone else's and a slightly different shape inside your head."

" I don't think that's at all nice, Mrs. Craggs. I tell you straight I don't."

" Never mind whether it's nice or not, my girl. It's the

truth. But what I want to know is : what was Mary Arthur saying to Jean-Artaban? "

Mrs. Milhorne looked away.

" Come on, now, I want to hear. You've told me she was saying something pretty strong and I mean to get to know what it was if I have to go on badgering you all day to get it out of you."

" Well, really."

" Yes, really."

" Well, I suppose I'll have to tell you then. Though I'm not sure that I should."

Mrs. Craggs waited.

" It was like this," said Mrs. Milhorne. " She was giving him a piece of her mind, a piece and a half. She told him that if he tried anything like that again she'd make such a fuss that it'd turn out to be him or her. My, you should have heard it. I wouldn't never have thought a little thing like that would have it in her."

" Ever tried anything like what again? " said Mrs. Craggs.

" Like you know."

" No, I don't know."

A faint, irregular blush showed on Mrs. Milhorne's sallow cheeks.

" Well, you know what Jean-Artaban's like, don't you? " she said.

" I know very well what he's like. He's like a devil most of the time. But which sort of a devil was he being this time? "

" It's difficult for me to say."

" Then you'll have to make your mind up to it. You heard this row, you can't keep it secret now."

Mrs. Milhorne sighed.

" I suppose I can't really."

" No, you can't. What was it he tried? Come on, out with it."

Mrs. Milhorne came out with it.

" Sex," she said.

" I guessed as much," said Mrs. Craggs.

She thought for a moment.

" It explains a bit of a spat I heard between them the other day," she said. " I never thought about it again till this moment."

She turned to Mrs. Milhorne.

" And she wasn't as willing as he'd thought she'd be? " she asked.

Mrs. Milhorne's blush deepened.

" Something like that," she said.

" So she was warning him off? "

" She was warning him all right. It would have done your heart good to hear it, except for the language of course."

Mrs. Milhorne contemplated the scene in her imagination.

Mrs. Craggs turned towards the door of Don Francisco's office.

" And now," she said, " you're going to repeat all that to the superintendent."

" What, me? "

" Yes, you."

" But I couldn't. I mean not to him. Not to Pryde of the Yard. Not all that."

" I don't see why not. It's plain enough he ought to know."

" But I can't tell him."

" Why not? "

Mrs. Milhorne looked down at her shoes. They had a twirling pattern of little punched holes.

" Well," she said, " it's him being him, like. You know, Pryde of the Yard. Famous. Somehow I couldn't bring myself to discuss a thing like that with a famous man. I just couldn't."

" Listen," said Mrs. Craggs, " he's a policeman, isn't he? He knows that men make passes at girls."

" Oh, I know that. I know that. Look at the Bed-hampton Strangler case that he pulled off so well. He'd have had to have known some pretty seamy facts of life for that. But it's somehow me talking to him about them that I can't imagine. It'd be like asking a film star if you could use their toilet."

" Well," said Mrs. Craggs, " if it's any help to you I can't see that the Bedhampton case makes him such a great man, for all the papers went on and on about it so. After all, the man was mad. Anyone could see that. He thought he was God Almighty. It should have been easy enough to spot him."

Mrs. Milhorne shook her head.

" I don't know about that," she said.

" Well," said Mrs. Craggs, " I do know about this. Pryde of the Yard or no Pryde of the Yard, he'll want to know what you've just told me and you're going straight in there to tell him."

And she opened the door and gave Mrs. Milhorne a slight but firm shove.

Mrs. Milhorne turned round for a moment as if she would rush back out. But Mrs. Craggs heard Super-

intendent Pryde pounce on her and ask her by name if
he could help.

" Well, I don't know," she heard Mrs. Milhorne
reply.

The simper in her voice was enough. Mrs. Craggs
sharply shut the door.

Mrs. Milhorne was in with the superintendent for only
five minutes.

When she came out Mrs. Craggs was waiting for her.
Mrs. Milhorne looked crestfallen.

" He didn't seem interested really," she said.

" Not interested? You're sure? "

" Yes, and I can see why, too."

" Oh, why? "

" It was something he said to that nice Sergeant
Jenkins."

" What did he say? "

" Something about the boot being on the other foot.
Do you know what, dear? I think he believes that the
person who did it wasn't trying to kill Mary Arthur at all.
They were trying to kill Jean-Artaban."

::   ::

And by next morning all the world shared Mrs. Milhorne's supposition. The papers were full of the fact that
they " understood " that the police were working on the
theory that this was " a murder case with the victim still
alive." It was the gossip of the hour.

Mrs. Craggs was sweeping the stage slowly and
methodically when a looming shadow fell across the path
of her broom. She glanced up to see Jean-Artaban. And
it was obvious at once that Jean-Artaban saw himself in a
new light.

He stood staring sombrely at Mrs. Craggs without saying a word.

Mrs. Craggs with the hint of a shrug went back to her sweeping. Jean-Artaban shifted his stance rather noisily and continued to regard her with the utmost baleful-ness.

At last he spoke.

" Well? "

Mrs. Craggs looked up.

" Oh, good morning, sir," she said. " I didn't hardly notice you. Have you been there long? "

" A certain amount of time."

Jean-Artaban paused.

" I was thinking. Thinking, my good Madame Craggs," he said.

" Oh, yes, sir. Very nice, too, I dare say."

" No," said Jean-Artaban.

He said it explosively.

" No, it was not very nice."

Mrs. Craggs resumed her sweeping.

" Do you know why it was not very nice, Madame Craggs? "

" I expect you'll tell me, sir."

Jean-Artaban shook his head gravely.

" I should not tell you, Madame Craggs," he replied. " You, above all, I should not tell."

" Still, I expect you will."

Jean-Artaban ignored this.

" And yet," he said, " I find myself impelled in some strange way to tell you all the same. To try an experiment. To take a risk."

Swish, swish, swish went Mrs. Craggs's broom.

" Yes, to take the risk of telling you that I was wondering if it was you who had set out to murder me."

" Oh, that," said Mrs. Craggs.

" Yes, that. Because I do not blink the possibility that it was you, Madame Craggs. There are ten people whom it could have been and you are one of the ten, Madame Craggs."

Mrs. Craggs did not look up.

Jean-Artaban resumed.

" There are some people," he said, " who would argue that because you and I have no social contacts it is unlikely that you are the one who tried to kill me. But I am not so foolish as that."

" No, sir."

" No, indeed. I know there are a thousand reasons why you might want to kill me."

" Oh, yes? "

" Or rather there are none."

" None, is it now, sir? "

" Well, yes, Madame Craggs, it must be none really. No one could have a real reason for wanting to kill me. If they have a thousand reasons it is because they have gone mad. And you, Madame Craggs, or your so elegant friend, Mrs. Milhorne, could go mad as easily as any of the other nine. I do not conceal that from myself."

" Well, that must make a change, sir."

" Make a change? I'm afraid I do not understand."

" Well, it seems to me, sir, that if you conceal from yourself the fact that people might want to kill you, you're concealing an 'ell of a lot."

Jean-Artaban's blond eyebrows rose in his wide forehead.

" People might want to kill me, Madame Craggs?
Except for a madman that is impossible."

" It seems only too possible to me, sir."

" But why, Madame Craggs? And who? But above all
who? "

" Would you like me to mention a few names, sir? "

" I most certainly would. This comes as a great shock
to me."

Jean-Artaban put out an expressive hand to quell any
protest.

" A shock," he said, " not because I expect to learn
that, outside your rather fevered imagination, anybody
wants to kill me—that is too laughable—but because it is
even possible that you should have been able to go about
thinking such a thing."

" Perhaps you'd rather I said nothing then, sir? "

" No, no. You must speak now, my good Madame
Craggs. This must all be brought out into the open. It is
most important. For your sake more than for mine."

Mrs. Craggs went on sweeping.

" Well, mention one name, one name."

" All right. How about Monsieur Paul? "

" Paul? My son? That he could want to kill me?
Ridiculous. I have been everything to that boy. I have
been more than a father. I have been a schoolmaster. A
friend. An employment agent even. No, no, my good
woman, he owes me such a debt of gratitude."

" You don't believe a debt of gratitude makes us feel
kindly disposed to people, do you, sir? "

" Oh, come, this is merest cynicism."

" Well, I call it something else. But believe you me, if
a debt of gratitude makes a person feel a bit resentful at

times, a debt of unwanted gratitude forced on someone by a father that they think ought to be just the opposite, that makes them feel murderous. You take my word for it."

"And so you think it was my son who tried to kill me?"

"I didn't say I thought that at all, sir."

"But——"

"I said he felt murderous towards you. That's a very different thing from saying he actually did all the things he would have had to have done to kill you in the way someone's supposed to have tried."

"So you withdraw your accusation?"

"I never made one, sir. I simply said that quite a lot of people might have wanted very well to kill you and I named Monsieur Paul as the first of them."

"It seems to me that you had better name the second. And pretty damn' quick."

"Well, how about Miss Glass then, sir?"

Jean-Artaban smiled.

Luxuriously.

"Now there, Madame Craggs," he said, "I concede you may be a little bit right. The poor tiresome creature. I dare say when I showed her that night during *Tosca* that she was no longer all that she had been to me she may have felt a little murderous."

He smirked.

"Happily," he said, "she is not one of the nine people in a position to have killed me."

"No, sir. I suppose it's lucky for her she isn't."

A quick frown appeared on Jean-Artaban's massive brow.

" But, tell me," he said, " how did you know of the relationship of myself and that poor foolish clinging creature? "

" I keep my eyes open, sir."

" Indeed? "

" And you don't do much about concealing things. In fact, that might well be why Madame Pivoine, if you'll excuse me saying so, could be feeling murderous towards you. Signorina Clarone did her best to tell her about you."

Jean-Artaban sighed.

" That shows how little you know of my dear sweet Alice," he said. " You don't think she minded about Clarissa, do you? She is not made that way, my dear Madame Craggs. Take the word of her husband for it. No, she knew. As you said, it could scarcely have been otherwise, even before my so delightful Margherita tried to tell her about it. She knew and she smiled."

" Just as you say, sir. But you were having an affair and she is your wife."

Jean-Artaban smiled.

" You have not been too convincing so far, Madame Craggs," he said.

" You want me to go on, sir? I could."

" Then do. By all means do."

" Well, there's Franz Prahler, sir."

" My good old friend, Franz. Yes? "

Jean-Artaban chuckled for rather a long time.

" Yes, Herr Prahler. There's something between the two of you, sir, though I don't pretend to know exactly what it is. But one thing's sure and certain : it's not friendship."

Jean-Artaban looked quizzical.

" And what sort of thing is this mysterious thing, my enigmatic friend? "

" It's nasty, I know that. I saw the look on his face the other day at rehearsal when you had that bit of a barney with him. You were baiting him about his singing, and then you added a remark which shut him up like a trap. It was something about knowing where he came from, or something like that. It may have seemed innocent enough, but I happened to be looking straight at Herr Prahler, and I know it wasn't so innocent."

" Poof," said Jean-Artaban. " Because sometimes it pleases me to tease a little that fat Austrian it does not mean he will murder me."

" This was something more than teasing."

" Ah, no, I assure you, really. All the world knows that he was an orphan boy from somewhere near Vienna. There is this little mystery about his origins which he so likes to build up. And I for a slight joke chose to pretend I knew more than I do. This is not a killing matter."

" Except that I saw his face."

Jean-Artaban shrugged.

" You are still not doing very well, Mrs. Craggs."

" Well, what about Don Francisco? I suppose you think he's the best friend you ever had? "

" I personally despise him. But there is no reason why he should not feel quite warm feelings to me."

" Only that you chased Madame Da Costa-O'Brien out of the theatre when everybody thought she was the only person in the world who would be able to sing the Goose Girl."

Jean-Artaban grinned.

" Yes," he said, " I was a bit—what do you say?—
naughty that day. But . . . A joke is a joke."

" And *Death of A Fat God* was going to make Don
Francisco's reputation at last. You knew that. You
knew it perfectly well."

But Jean-Artaban was not disconcerted.

" My dear Madame Craggs, nothing, positively
nothing, could make Don Francisco's reputation. Take
my word for that."

" That's got nothing to do with it. He thought this was
his chance, and he saw you breaking it up. For nothing.
For a joke."

" But in any case Don Francisco has not the force to
commit a murder. Much less try to murder me."

" Then shall I tell you who has? "

" By all means."

Jean-Artaban bowed.

" Your former wife."

" Ah, my poor Margherita. Certainly she would be
delighted to hear you say she is a murderess. That is how
she likes to think of herself, the poor silly creature. But
underneath . . . "

A pitying smile.

" Underneath it is a little lamb, a little baa-lamb."

" Oh."

The cry from behind the painted walls of the Pasha
Selim's house rang out like a whole chorus of Valkyries.

The Pasha's front door was flung open.

Standing in the threshold was Margherita Clarone.

CHAPTER XVI

"OH, OH, OH," said Margherita Clarone, "so it is a little baa-lamb, is it? You thought I was not there, Jean-Artaban, and that you could say such things about me. But you were wrong. I was there. I heard."

She tossed her luxuriant black curls and looked scornfully down at the great bulk of her former husband from the pretty little flight of steps that led from the Pasha Selim's house to his garden.

Jean-Artaban's large face remained more or less impassive though a tiny spark of malice showed in his eyes.

"Yes," he said, "I was discussing with this good lady who it might have been who tried to murder me. We were agreeing that a person of your emotional immaturity could hardly be considered a suspect."

"Ah, yes," said Margherita, "I have heard of this notion that you were the intended victim, Jean-Artaban."

She shrugged.

"Well," she said, "if it is true I am glad the person failed to kill you."

"Glad?"

Jean-Artaban seemed surprised.

Margherita, who had begun the descent of the steps of the Pasha's house with a finely careless air, looked up triumphantly.

"Yes," she said, "glad. Glad because you are still there for me to hurt in my own way and my own time."

Her eyes shone.

193

N

" Perhaps I shall kill you," she went on, " or perhaps I shall find a better way of making you suffer. But do not think you will escape. I have waited for my moment and I think it is growing near. Then you will know what it is to have offended Margherita Clarone."

" Bah," said Jean-Artaban, " you poor thing. You cannot touch me in any way. You know that."

Standing towering on the half-swept stage he did indeed look invincible, immovable.

But hardly had he boasted of his invulnerability when a sudden sound made him start and look round in an almost hunted manner.

It was the quiet New England voice of his wife calling his name from somewhere out of sight in the wings.

" Yes, I am here on the stage, my dear," he called back. " I will come to you. Where are you? "

He began to move in the direction of the Pasha Selim's door but at the same moment his wife emerged from behind the fig-tree in the garden.

" Stop. Stay right where you are, Jean-Artaban," she called.

Her voice, quiet though it was, carried well. Jean-Artaban stopped with one foot on the Pasha's steps and stood rooted to the spot as if he was a rather eccentric part of the set.

" I could see us just chasing each other in and out these fearsome flats and things all the rest of the morning," Alice said in a more conversational tone.

Jean-Artaban, discovering that he was not being apprehended for a particular offence, relaxed and turned towards her.

" But, my dearest one," he said, " why should you have

to chase your great bear of a husband? You have only to say that you want him and he will come."

"I thought you might be here on business," Alice answered. "And, though it might be nice for me to have you leave a rehearsal right in the middle just because I'd dropped my handkerchief or something, it isn't a thing other people would appreciate too much."

"Other people," Jean-Artaban said.

"Well, they exist, my pet. And if what the papers said this morning is true, one other person seems to have been pretty determined to make an impression on you."

"Good morning, my dear," said Margherita suddenly and loudly.

"Why, hallo there. Is this a rehearsal after all then?"

"No, no," Margherita said. "It just so happened that both of us had come to the theatre for different reasons. But you are quite right in what you were saying to poor Jean-Artaban. He will learn one day that if he rides over people for ever one of them will get up and strike him."

Alice looked at her sharply.

"Well," she said, "I only hope that they have the sense to realise that Jean-Artaban says much more than he means before somebody else gets hurt. That poor, poor girl."

She sat down on the low wall of the Pasha's garden.

"I'm trying to persuade myself the papers are talking a lot of nonsense," she said.

She sat for a moment watching Mrs. Craggs who had quietly returned to her broom. She looked openly worried.

Margherita stood looking at her.

"My dear," she said, "all the same you should not

take too light a view of this great bear's antics. They are sometimes very serious."

Alice looked up at her and smiled.

"Well," she said, "I can't somehow bring myself to believe that he does the sort of thing that would make someone want to kill him."

"Pah," said Margherita, "how you came to marry him I will never understand. You don't know him. You don't know him one bit."

"I think the facts are in my favour," Alice said.

There was a new sharpness in her tone.

"Facts? What facts? This isn't a question of facts. This is a question of feelings."

Alice smiled a little wryly.

"The facts I referred to are the outward signs of the feelings you are so interested in," she said.

"I don't——"

"I mean the fact that you were married to him and are not, and that I am married to him and intend to stay that way."

Margherita tossed her luxuriant black hair.

"Oh, yes," she said, "you think that I lost him because I didn't understand him, and that you are keeping him because you do. But let me tell you that you couldn't be more wrong. I got rid of him because at last I had come to understand him through and through and knew that there was no hope for him. And you, you are keeping him because you obstinately refuse to open your eyes."

"I think not," Alice said.

There was a stiffening of dignity in the three short words.

"Oh, you think not."

Nothing could stem Margherita's torrents.

"You think not. You bury your head in the sand like the what do you call it—the *struzzo*—and you think not. But one day you will get a terrible awakening. I tell you that this man, this pig, he does things which people will never forgive him for. It is no wonder someone tried to kill him. He has made enemies to the death all over the world. He thinks of nobody but himself, ever. He deserves to die."

"My dear," Alice said.

Her quiet voice was in total contrast to the almost shrieking violence of the Italian.

"My dear, aren't you just a little exaggerating?"

"Of couse she is."

Jean-Artaban had been left out of things too long.

"No," Margherita shouted. "No, I will prove it to you."

"My Alice, you will not believe her. She is crazy. She wants me still. She is mad with jealousy."

But such arguments were unlikely to appeal to Alice. She stood up with a faint smile on her lips.

"No, Jean-Artaban," she said, "even your vanity should not permit you to believe that."

She turned to Margherita.

"But to some extent Jean-Artaban is right," she said. "I guess there's not much point in carrying on with this discussion."

She linked her arm through Jean-Artaban's.

"You know," she said, "if you people really aren't rehearsing or anything, you can take me for a drive, Jean-Artaban. It's a lovely day. All that golden sunshine. When I'd never been outside of New England I didn't ever understand what that poem—the one about mists and mellow fruitfulness, you know—was about. And now I've got the chance I can't see too much of it."

Leaning a little on her husband's arm she began to walk across the stage in the direction of the stage-door corridor and the workaday streets of Flinwich suffused with the transient glow of the autumn sunshine.

" No," Margherita shouted again.

She had stood watching Jean-Artaban and his wife in their leisurely progress, and then had thrown back her head and let out this single loud explosion of protest.

" Ah, no," she said, " I cannot let you go on in ignorance like this. You will hear if I have to follow you out into the street and shout it out for all the world to share."

Alice and Jean-Artaban stopped.

It would have been absurd in face of this volley of sound to have walked on pretending that nothing was happening.

Alice dropped Jean-Artaban's arm and turned half back to look at Margherita.

" My dear," she said, " let me persuade you not to go on with this."

" You shall not. You shall hear. You will learn what this man you have married is like."

Margherita was breathing through her distended nostrils like a war-horse.

" I will tell you one thing only," she said. " One thing. But something he did just a few days ago. Not history. Not something that rankles from the days of our marriage. But something from the days of yours."

" This is absurd," Jean-Artaban said.

He took hold of his wife's arm.

"No, dear," said Alice quietly. "We had better hear it out."

"Ah, that is better," Margherita said. "Now you will learn something about this man you married with so little thought."

"Oh, no," said Alice, "that I did not do."

"Well, we shall see. Let me tell you about your so good husband and the poor foolish Clarissa Glass."

"Only that," Alice said. "Why, I guess you told me all about that before."

"Ah, but—— "

"No," Alice interrupted. "Let me tell you something. At the time when you came out with your precious titbit there was half the theatre around so I pretended I had hardly understood. But I understood very well. And now that we're a bit more private— "

She glanced quickly at Mrs. Craggs, who had gone through the Pasha's garden and was prosaically dusting the fantasticated boat which during the course of the opera glided up to and away from a tiny quay in the background.

"Now that we are a little more private, let me explain to you that you weren't telling me anything I didn't know perfectly well."

"Ah, you knew," said Margherita.

She did not seem as abashed as she might have been.

"Yes, I knew."

"Then did you also know this?" Margherita retorted. "Did you know about the savage way your kind husband finished that little affair?"

Alice looked puzzled.

"I thought not," Margherita went on. "I thought

that nobody could bring themselves to tell you the nasty facts to your face. All the world is always kind to you. But I will tell you. I said just now that I would like to hurt you, Jean-Artaban, and I see my chance."

" Don't believe her," Jean-Artaban said.

" Oh, there were witnesses enough," said Margherita. " There were hundreds of witnesses. The whole theatre full. All of them saw your delightful husband when he was playing Scarpia get up and live again after Tosca had killed him. He humiliated that poor Clarissa in front of a whole audience of people. That was his way of telling her the affair was at an end."

Slowly Alice sat down on the low wall again.

She looked at Jean-Artaban.

" It's true? " she said.

" But—— "

Jean-Artaban began some protest.

Alice turned round and spoke loudly to Mrs. Craggs.

" Is it true my husband brought himself to life again as Scarpia? " she asked.

" Yes, it's true," Mrs. Craggs said.

Alice's face had lost its apple-red colour.

She looked beaten down.

Jean-Artaban launched into his flood of protestations. His wife did not appear to hear.

CHAPTER XVII

" I'VE BEEN READING the papers," Mrs. Milhorne said to Mrs. Craggs later that morning.

" Oh, yes ? "

" Yes. 'Course I don't agree with them putting all those murders in. But when it's one on your doorstep like, the way I see it is you've got to read it."

Mrs. Craggs smiled to herself.

" Why don't you agree with them putting in the murders? " she said.

Mrs. Milhorne looked shocked.

" Why," she said, " it's downright nasty."

" It's life."

" Well, it may be. But there's parts of life they've no call to put in the papers."

" People want to read about them."

" Well, they shouldn't. It isn't nice."

Mrs. Milhorne returned with an unusual access of vigour to polishing the brass handles of the left-hand set of foyer entrance doors.

But her disapproval of Mrs. Craggs's vulgarity could not outweight her desire to discuss what she had read in the despised papers.

" I see they think it was Jean-Artaban who was meant to be murdered," she said at last. " I told you as much yesterday."

" Yes," said Mrs. Craggs.

" But what I can't understand is," Mrs. Milhorne said, " whether it makes a difference over who could have done it. Except it couldn't be Jean-Artaban himself. I see that."

" As far as I can tell it doesn't make any difference at all," Mrs. Craggs said. " Anyone could have got to the weights without being seen. Just as before."

" Just as before? "

Mrs. Craggs looked patiently at Mrs. Milhorne.

"It was bound to be just as before, wasn't it?" she said. "The weights were taken off and the god's car fell. The fact that it fell empty and hit Mary Arthur instead of falling with Jean-Artaban in makes no difference."

Mrs. Milhorne considered.

"I suppose you're right really," she said.

"I know I'm right."

"And I suppose that was why all that measuring and pointing and whatnot went on on the stage yesterday."

"'Course it was. They had to find out who could get down to the weights and back out of sight quick enough. And they wanted to know how much each of us could see from the places we were in."

"I couldn't see a thing in that dressing-room."

Mrs. Craggs sighed.

"I know you couldn't, dear," she said. "But not everybody was in a dressing-room like you and me. Some of them were out and they might have been able to see if anyone was moving about."

"Oh, that explains it then."

"Explains what?"

"What that nice Sergeant Jenkins was telling me. I couldn't understand a word of it at the time, but of course I didn't let on."

"He was telling you what they were doing?"

"Yes. He said it didn't do them a blind bit of good, all that work, though."

"Oh. Why not?"

"Nobody could see anything. He showed me it all and I see what he meant now. He was ever so nice about it."

"And what did he say?"

" Well, let me think."

Mrs. Milhorne stopped polishing the handles and fell into deep thought.

After a little Mrs. Craggs came across from the right-hand pair of doors and set to work on the half-finished handles of Mrs. Milhorne's pair.

" Yes," said Mrs. Milhorne, " it was like this. The fly gallery, as they call it, runs right through the whole top of the back of the theatre with the two staircases going up to it in each corner, and the ropes with the brakes are plumb in the middle, so that anyone going down either staircase could get to the weights down below equally well."

" Thanks for nothing," said Mrs. Craggs.

" Well, you asked me what Sergeant Jenkins had told me, and that was what he did. And I must say I followed him a treat up to that bit. It was only when he told me where everybody was that I began to get muddled."

" What did he tell you? "

" Well, that poor Mary Arthur was standing just by the temple entrance waiting to go on stage and so naturally she wouldn't have seen anybody creeping along under the gallery right behind her."

" Well, that's clear enough."

" And who next? Oh, yes. Jean-Artaban. Well, he was standing on the little platform at the end of the cat-walk just next to the god's car. And he was looking down on the stage side of the scenery waiting till the last minute to step into the car."

" I suppose he was right to make such a fuss as it turned out."

" Well, of course. He said he was never going to get into that car until the last moment, and it was well for him that he stuck to it."

" You know Jean-Artaban," Mrs. Craggs said, " if he'd gone and announced a thing like that, he'd stick to it all right. Wouldn't dare to risk losing face by changing his mind."

A thought struck her.

" But I don't recall ever hearing him say any such thing," she said. " Not in so many words."

" Oh, don't you, dear? Well, you can take it from me he said it all right. Made quite a fuss about it."

" Just to you was this? "

" Oh, no, dear."

Mrs. Milhorne looked at Mrs. Craggs with pity.

" No, dear," she said, " it was to everyone. I'm surprised you weren't there. But I dare say you'd gone off to do a bit of work like."

" I dare say. I do do a bit of work from time to time."

Mrs. Craggs breathed on Mrs. Milhorne's set of handles and gave them a last rub.

It was a long, hard rub and when she had finished it she looked distinctly pleased with herself.

" Come up a treat really," Mrs. Milhorne said.

" Yes," said Mrs. Craggs.

She turned to her friend.

" Well," she said, " and what did your Sergeant Jenkins have to say about Madame Alice Towell Pivoine for instance? "

" Well, let me see. Oh, yes. She was in her husband's dressing-room, of course. So she couldn't have seen what was happening any more than what we could."

" All right. Well, who next? "

" Franz Prahler was in his dressing-room, too, of course, and so was Margherita Clarone. If they're both telling the truth, the sergeant said, neither of them could have seen anything. But if one of them was lying they could have been creeping along to the end of the dressing-room gallery, either on the ladies' side or the gentlemen's according to which was which, and creeping down the iron stairs and along to the weights."

" You're being very clear so far, dear."

Mrs. Milhorne assumed a dreamy look.

" It's all coming back to me," she said.

" Well, go on."

" Yes. Well, there are the three who don't count, of course : young Albert Sime because he fainted dead away and Monsieur Paul and Don Francisco. Monsieur Paul was playing the piano and Don Francisco was sitting out in the front. So that leaves us with just Madame Glistanova and her husband. Well, with the way she moves so slow and being so old, they don't reckon on her being one of the ones who could have done it and got back away from the weights quick enough. But she was there sitting on that golden throne thing and he was with her of course. No—— "

Mrs. Milhorne stopped and frowned.

" That's where I got muddled," she announced.

An air of triumphant vindication.

" I can tell you where he was," said Mrs. Craggs.

" Oh, can you, dear? I'd be obliged if you could. I'd like to get it all straight in my own mind."

" He was in the gents'."

Mrs. Milhorne looked sharply in the other direction.

" Well," said Mrs. Craggs, " wasn't that what Sergeant Jenkins told you? It was what Superintendent Pryde told me."

" The sergeant didn't tell me in so many words," Mrs. Milhorne replied.

She spoke from a great distance.

" But that was what he meant? "

" If you must. Only the sergeant, I'm happy to say, put it more nicely."

" But he told you that Mr. Einfalt was in that gents' off the corridor going to the stage door? "

" Oh, no."

" No? What do you mean ' No '? "

" I mean he couldn't have been there."

" But why ever not? "

Mrs. Milhorne looked down at her twirly-patterned shoes.

" Well, you see," she said, " I locked it up."

" Locked it up? "

" It's all a bit embarrassing," Mrs. Milhorne said.

" It also happens to prove someone was lying. Out with it, my girl."

" You mean it shows Mr. Einfalt wasn't where he said he was? I hadn't thought of that, not knowing properly where he was supposed to have been."

" Well, why was the gents' locked? "

" I hardly like to say."

Mrs. Milhorne sighed.

" It was like this, you see," she went on, " it happened to come out in conversation one day with Mr. Strutt that he didn't—Well, that he didn't ever do very much about cleaning up that place."

" The gents'? "

" Well, yes. He thought the work was beneath him, in a manner of speaking."

" I know."

" Well, I didn't like to think what sort of state it, the place, might get into. So—Well, so I took to turning a key in the lock at nights. So it wouldn't be used too much. One of the keys on my bunch fitted a treat."

" I see. Well, it looks as though you'd better go along and have another chat with the super."

Unexpectedly Mrs. Milhorne displayed none of her former reluctance.

" Yes," she said, " I do think I'll have to go and have a little chat with Pryde of the Yard. And I think he'll be rather glad to hear what I have to say this time."

" Of course he will. When he catches someone out telling a lie he's beginning to get somewhere. When he hears that that gents' was locked, he'll bounce up like a rubber ball. You see if he doesn't."

" Oh, I don't think I'll need to mention that."

" Not mention—— But that's the whole point. Why, you—— "

" If you'll excuse me, dear. I admit that that business did seem important a few minutes ago. But that was before the case was solved."

" Solved? Have you gone barmy or something? "

Mrs. Milhorne's face certainly did have a curious, rapt look.

" No," she said, " not barmy. Just inspired."

She looked pityingly at Mrs. Craggs.

" Yes," she said, " I've just this moment seen it all. Seen it in one single flash."

She shook her head wisely.

" You know, dear," she went on, " it isn't always brains as does it in this world. There's such a thing as insight as well. I've just had a blinding flash of insight."

" Oh, have you, dear? Well, what did it tell you? "

" Madame Glistanova. Madame Glistanova. That's what it told me."

" That she's a killer? Are you saying that Madame Glistanova is a killer? You must be mad."

Mrs. Milhorne assumed an expression of extreme cunning.

" Well, dear," she said, " I'm not telling you that she killed Jean-Artaban."

Mrs. Craggs's face under her uncompromising hat became frankly incredulous.

" I thought—— "

Mrs. Milhorne smiled serenely.

" I'm telling you she killed Mary Arthur," she said. " It was Mary Arthur after all that was meant to be killed."

Mrs. Craggs's look of incredulity did not lessen.

" Go on," she said, " what makes you believe that? How do you work it out? "

" Oh," said Mrs. Milhorne, " my mind doesn't work things out. I don't have to go into a lot of reasoning. I just see. It was as if I'd completely forgotten that it was Jean-Artaban that was meant to be the victim. I just thought of Madame Glistanova and something about her flashed into my mind, and then I realised why she wanted to kill that poor innocent girl."

" You'd better tell me," said Mrs. Craggs.

Mrs. Milhorne tossed her head.

" Well, all right, dear, if you like," she said. " It'll be a sort of rehearsal for what I tell to Pryde of the Yard."

She drew a deep breath.

" It was like this," she said. " I'd just told you how the police thought that Madame Glistanova couldn't really be counted as being a suspect because of her being so old and tottering about from one place to another like on her stick, when suddenly as you were saying something or other I remembered."

" Remembered what? "

Mrs. Milhorne blushed lightly in passing.

" I remembered the way she came up to me just after the murder was done," she said. " You recall I was a bit overcome at the sight. We haven't all got nerves of iron, you know. And I may have been a trifle hysterical. Well, she went up those iron stairs like a tiger and came up to me and gave me such a blow. I dare say the bruise is there yet under me *Fragrance de Paris*."

Mrs. Craggs stepped nearer and looked at the layer of powder dusting Mrs. Milhorne's sallow cheeks.

" There's something in what you say," she admitted. " I dare say in moments of stress the old lady can move a sight faster than she does in the ordinary way. It means she could have done it, as no doubt the superintendent very well knows. But what in heaven's name makes you think she would possibly want to? "

" Jealousy," said Mrs. Milhorne.

She looked blandly at Mrs. Craggs.

" Jealousy," she repeated. " That's what done it. Of course, you can tell at once that underneath that calm exterior she's a creature of passion. I dare say a lot of it's burnt out now, her being so old like. But I bet that in

o

her day it was there all right. And there she was the only
person in the world who'd ever sung the Goose Girl in
Death of A Fat God and suddenly out of the blue comes
this young thing and everybody says she can sing it just
as well if not better. No wonder she came down hot-foot
to offer her advice. Advice, indeed, if I was going to get
that sort of advice I wouldn't expect to be long on this
earth."

" But no."

The explosive sound came from behind the two
cleaners lost in their discussion.

They both whirled round.

Through the pair of entrance doors that Mrs. Craggs
had left open after polishing their handles had come
Heinrich Einfalt and his wife. It was the insignificant
little Heinrich who had exploded with such indignation.

" It is all right, Heinrich. There is no need to get so
angry."

Xaria Glistanova leant on her silver-headed cane and
looked from her little husband, the blood already draining
away from his face, across to the two cleaners.

" We did not mean to overhear," she said. " We
happened to see the doors open and it is rather easier for
me to come in this way than to go round by the stage
door."

Mrs. Milhorne tossed her lank hair.

" Some of us can move quick enough when we've a
mind to," she said.

Xaria Glistanova smiled a little.

" Yes," she said, " of course I moved quickly when you
quite naturally lost control after that poor girl had been

killed. I see that you must have taken that into account in your indictment of me just now."

" You know very well I did," said Mrs. Milhorne.

She looked suspicious, but less certain of herself.

Again Xaria Glistanova smiled.

" I guessed it," she said, " I did not know it. We heard only the very last of your remarks."

She glanced down at her husband.

" I am afraid Heinrich would have interrupted at once had he heard any of your accusation," she said. " He is very quick to defend my interests."

She sighed.

" I only wish he was sometimes a little quicker to defend his own," she said.

" His own," said Mrs. Milhorne.

Her indignation seemed to be reviving.

" Never mind all that, dear," Mrs. Craggs broke in. " You leave me to explain to Madame how all this happened. You've got to go and do what we were talking about before. Remember? "

Mrs. Milhorne looked puzzled.

" Well," said Mrs. Craggs cheerfully, " it's got to be a surprise for him, hasn't it? I mean, there's a bit of a hurry, isn't there, if he isn't to know in advance? "

Mrs. Milhorne looked at her.

The working out of the enigma could be seen going on, painfully slowly, on her face.

In the meantime Madame Glistanova was beginning to look a little put out by the mysterious by-play.

But suddenly something dawned on Mrs. Milhorne's countenance.

" Oh, yes," she said. " He mustn't know beforehand. Of course. You're right, dear."

She turned to Xaria Glistanova and her husband.

" Well," she said brightly, " I must be off then. Ta ta for now."

She turned and went.

Madame Glistanova looked at her retreating back sombrely.

" You'll excuse her, I'm sure," said Mrs. Craggs. " The fact of the matter is that it's someone's birthday—Mr. Strutt, the stage doorkeeper, as a matter of fact—and we were going to get him a little present as a surprise. And I was afraid she wouldn't get it in time."

" Indeed," said Madame Glistanova.

Mrs. Craggs blushed.

" But I ought to be apologising for her saying what she did about you, instead of going on about all that," she said. " The truth is she gets very overwrought at times. You know that yourself from the way she behaved when she saw that poor girl's body. But she oughtn't to have said all that, when it's plain it's not true."

Xaria Glistanova looked at her sharply.

" It is plain to you, is it? " she asked.

" Well, of course."

" I see. And why do you think that? "

Mrs. Craggs looked at her squarely.

" Because one's only got to hear you speak to know that vanity doesn't come into it with you," she said. " The whole idea is quite ridiculous. I don't suppose you were even vain about your voice when you were actually singing the Goose Girl, let alone all these years later. You're not like the majority of singers I've come across in the theatre here, and I'd have thought even Flo Milhorne could have seen that."

"You are quite right. You are quite right."

Heinrich Einfalt having adjusted himself to his normal quietness after his initial outburst now broke in excitedly again.

"You are quite right. She was different from almost every other singer I have met. And in my time I have met them all. I tell you : it is only the truly great who are not vain of their voices."

He turned and looked up at his wife, bent and aged and thin as a skeleton.

"She was proud of her voice, mind you," he lisped. "She was proud of it as a man might be proud of his country. But there was not one atom of vanity in her for herself."

"Well," said Mrs. Craggs, "anyone with half an eye in their heads could have seen that."

Xaria Glistanova smiled her quiet smile, the corners of her mouth moving a little and a tiny gleam showing in her eyes.

"But nevertheless," she said, "the fact remains that under some extraordinary stimulus I suppose I could have got away from the weights quickly enough after pulling them off. I gather that not much force would be needed to tip them off the holding bars."

She smiled again.

"But perhaps the pattern of the weights has changed since I was last in a theatre," she said.

"I don't suppose so as a matter of fact," Mrs. Craggs said. "They could certainly be tipped off the bars pretty easily."

"But this is nonsense," muttered Heinrich Einfalt.

"I suppose it is the sort of nonsense a policeman has to take into account," his wife replied.

She shrugged her bony shoulders under the black shawl.

"But we will hardly let it worry us," she said.

She turned to Mrs. Craggs again.

"Tell me," she said, "are so many suspicions being discussed all over the theatre? Who else is being pilloried?"

Her eyes glittered.

Mrs. Craggs was not discomposed.

"It's simple enough, so they tell me," she said. "When the poor girl was killed the theatre was completely locked up except for the stage door. And anyone passing through that had to go in front of the eagle-eyed gaze of Mr. Strutt. You talk to him and you'll find out how easy it would be to get past that. Well, there were only eleven of us in the theatre at that time. So they say it was bound to be one of us."

"I see."

Xaria Glistanova considered for a brief moment.

"I find I do not know who these eleven unfortunates are," she said.

Mrs. Craggs's mouth hardened.

"I don't think you can call one of them unfortunate," she replied.

"No, I suppose not, though one never knows what has driven some wretch to do a thing like that. But, tell me, besides Heinrich and myself, who were the other nine?"

"Well, there was Monsieur and Madame Pivoine and young Monsieur Paul. Then there was Don Francisco out in front and Herr Prahler, who was in his dressing-room, and Signorina Clarone in hers, as well as myself and Mrs. Milhorne and young Albert Sime on the brakes up in the fly gallery."

" Thank you," said Madame Glistanova.

She stood thinking.

Then she spoke.

" That is an extraordinary thing," she said. " Your numbers tally, but there was one other person in the theatre just a few seconds before the car fell."

Mrs. Craggs looked at her.

" Another? "

" Yes. I saw her myself."

" Who was it? "

Xaria Glistanova ceased to lean on her silver-knobbed stick.

" It was that young soprano," she said, " Clarissa Glass. Quite a reasonable voice but no actress."

CHAPTER XVIII

MRS. CRAGGS stood looking at the thin form of Xaria Glistanova.

" You saw Clarissa Glass in the theatre just before Mary Arthur was killed? " she said.

" Yes, I did."

" But then why didn't you tell the police? I'm sorry, but I just don't understand."

" I did not tell the police simply because I did not realise they were under the impression that only those people who had appeared immediately after the car fell were likely to have committed the crime. Indeed, I thought they were more likely not to have been guilty. I had imagined the guilty one had fled."

Madame Glistanova shrugged.

"They asked me quite a lot of questions about the people I had seen just after the crime," she went on, "but I thought they were simply concerned to establish everybody's whereabouts so that they could determine which areas of the theatre were free from surveillance. They never actually asked me whether I had seen anybody else."

"Well," said Mrs. Craggs, "they'll want to know straight away. This puts a different look on things."

"How do you mean?" asked Heinrich Einfalt.

He glanced solicitiously at his wife.

"I mean that if someone was here and has said nothing about it, things look pretty black for them," said Mrs. Craggs. "There's no use blinking the facts. Especially as Miss Glass might be said to have good reason for feeling badly about Monsieur Pivoine."

"And why was this?" asked Madame Glistanova. "I have missed being told all about the intrigues that go on."

"She had been his mistress," Mrs. Craggs said.

With blunt relish.

"And he'd got tired of her," she added, "as he gets tired of them all sooner or later. So he let her know it by coming to life again when he was singing Scarpia to her Tosca."

"Yes," said Madame Glistanova. "I did hear something about that. It was an appallingly cruel thing to do."

" But not cruel enough to justify murder," Mrs. Craggs said. " I wouldn't have that."

" I believe there are opera singers who would disagree with you," said Madame Glistanova. " But I was not suggesting that they are right. No, if Clarissa Glass has done this terrible thing, it is from being spurned by her lover. One sees that."

" And it is only if," said Mrs. Craggs. " What you say was no proof."

" No, indeed," Xaria Glistanova said. " I did not see her even go near those weights. I caught one glimpse of her, outlined against the light coming from the stage. And then she vanished into the darkness. The crash of the falling car came a little after that."

She sighed.

" I am afraid I do not know quite how long," she said. " The superintendent will not be pleased with me. But I am an old woman and time sometimes gets very vague for me."

Mrs. Craggs's eyes lit up.

" Perhaps you were mistaken then? " she said. " Could this all have happened some time before? Perhaps Miss Glass had left well before the car came down? "

Xaria Glistanova shook her head.

" Ah, no," she said. " I make some mistakes, but my ear is still what it was. I could show you the exact notes being played the moment Clarissa Glass was in my view. You will find they do not come much before the moment of the disaster."

She bowed her head for a moment. The skinny hands holding the silver knob of the cane tightened.

Heinrich Einfalt stepped quickly forward and supported her elbow.

She turned to him.

" Thank you, my dear," she said. " But I am all right."

She looked at Mrs. Craggs.

" The superintendent has asked to see us," she said. " We will have unexpected news for him. Thank goodness I am not the one who has to assess its worth."

Mrs. Craggs watched her walk slowly away into the auditorium with her little husband sidling along half a pace behind her.

::   ::

It appeared that Superintendent Pryde between giving interviews to the squad of crime reporters who more or less constantly besieged Don Francisco's office had begun another extensive round of questioning. In the course of her work Mrs. Craggs met all the others who had been in the theatre at the moment Mary Arthur was killed.

She was busy with the vacuum cleaner working her way along the rows of the stalls when the sound of sharp voices on the stage behind her made her turn round.

Franz Prahler and Clarissa Glass were standing bang in the middle of the stage facing each other angrily.

Luckily for Mrs. Craggs the vacuum cleaner had been renewed at the beginning of the season. It purred discreetly. She was able to hear the row on the stage every bit as clearly as her passionate interest in human nature, preferably getting a little raw, required.

The words that had caused her to turn round had been Franz's.

" Oh, so it's you," he had said loudly and furiously. " It

is you come back to gloat over the place where you killed Mary Arthur."

" What the hell do you mean by that? "

If Franz was in an awkward mood, so obviously was Clarissa.

" I tell you what I mean by that, *liebling*. Don't think Franz Prahler is ashamed of what he says. I mean you've been found out. It's all over the place. Everybody knows. You were in the theatre all the time, and you killed her. You killed the girl who was going to prove that Franz Prahler was the greatest teacher of singing the world had ever known, a new de Reszke. And you had to kill the pupil he brought up from not even being able to sing in tune."

" What bloody nonsense."

When Clarissa lost her temper her accent betrayed her humble Birmingham origins more clearly than ever.

" I tell you it is all over everywhere," Franz shouted. " Why haven't the police arrested you I should like to know."

" Arrested me? What the bloody hell do you think they would arrest me for? "

" For killing her, for killing my little Mary Arthur."

" Only it so happens that I didn't kill her."

" You did. You did."

The little tenor was bouncing so fiercely with rage that Mrs. Craggs laid down the vacuum cleaner, leaving it still running, and began to go sideways along the close-set rows of tip-up seats in the direction of the pass door to the stage. It looked as if she might have to intervene.

" I did not," Clarissa shouted back at Franz. " Now shut up and leave me to go my own way."

" I will not leave you. How do I know that you are not running away from the police? If they haven't arrested you they ought to have done. You will stay where you are."

Clarissa made an attempt to get past the stocky little Austrian. But he was quick on his feet and instantly placed himself in her path with outstretched arms.

" No, you don't, *liebling*," he said.

Clarissa looked at him furiously.

" Listen," she said, " I did not murder your little Mary Arthur. Why should I? I'd only seen the kid about three times. She seemed nice enough, even if she was inclined to think that she was the only one in the whole world who could sing. But I wasn't going to kill her for that."

" It was not her you meant to kill. You cannot fool me. I tell you : everything is known about you."

" Oh, it is, is it? Well, thank you very much."

" Yes, I tell you. All about your love-making with Jean-Artaban, the foul pig, it is known. And everybody saw what he did to you in *Tosca*. Of course you tried to kill him. But you killed my Mary Arthur instead."

" Now listen to me, you dirty little bastard. I may have done what I have done with Jean-Artaban, and it's quite certain he did something unforgivable in *Tosca*. But it so happens I didn't try to kill him, see. It just never occurred to me. And that's all there is to it."

" Oh, no, it isn't. What were you doing sneaking and skulking in the theatre at the time of the murder if you were not going round to take off the weights on the god's car? Tell me that."

" I most certainly will not. What I was doing is my own private business and I mean to see it stays that way."

" Oh, private business. Of course it is. You wouldn't want all the world to know you were killing my poor Mary Arthur. No wonder it was private business."

" It had nothing to do with your poor Mary Arthur."

" Oh, yes. I believe that, thank you. Tell that to the police."

Clarissa grinned suddenly.

" It so happens that's exactly what I have done," she said. " I've just come from doing exactly and precisely that. And the superintendent sent the Press boys off on some fools' errand and then held the door open for me and bowed me out."

" You lie. You lie altogether. I will not let you go."

Franz began to advance towards Clarissa in a decidedly menacing way. And although Clarissa was the taller and looked as if with her lithe figure and easy carriage she could give a good account of herself, Mrs. Craggs thought it was definitely time to nip across to the pass door, run quickly up the short flight of steps that led to the stage level and do what she could do to part the combatants.

But her efforts were unnecessary.

Before she had even reached the small inconspicuous door tucked into a corner next to the edge of the orchestra pit, Don Francisco came hurrying on to the stage.

"No. No. No. No. No," he said. "Not more troubling."

He planted himself firmly between Clarissa and Franz and looked at them each in turn rapidly, ready to quell whatever revolt might spring up first.

When he saw that his intervention had produced faint expressions of relief on the faces of both potential combatants his attention sank back to his own troubles.

" First I am taken away my own offices," he said.

" Then I am always questioning with the polices. Now is my artists fighting. It is the most bad."

" Well, I can't say I'm that sorry for you," Clarissa answered. " I've got troubles of my own. Can't you control this man? "

" Control me? Control Franz Prahler? It would take a better director than him to control me. If I want to be uncontrolled, uncontrolled I will be."

Franz looked round the gloomy, half-lit theatre.

" That is what this place needs," he said. " Some excitement. Something uncontrolled."

He pounced forward and thrust his face into Don Francisco's.

" I think it might be a good idea if I pull your hair," he said.

Don Francisco backed away.

Franz advanced.

A glint of wild, elfin, bitter humour shone in his eyes.

Don Francisco backed away with haste.

Franz, evidently determined to vent his bad temper to the full, advanced on him rapidly.

" I forbidding," said Don Francisco.

As if he knew there was no chance of being heeded.

Franz, with a savage smile, jumped forward. He seized a handful of Don Francisco's black curls and tugged.

" There," he said. " There, that will teach you to have murders in your theatre."

He tugged again.

" There. That will teach you to look after the artists entrusted to your care."

Another tug. And a sharp, short scream from Don Francisco.

" There. That will teach you to let the products of years of master teaching be killed. Years of master teaching. Who else could have discovered that voice buried so deep there ? "

He tugged longer and harder.

Don Francisco screamed longer and harder. Much longer and much, much harder.

There was the sound of running feet.

In a few moments a small crowd had collected on the stage. Franz and his victim were encircled. They stood looking at each other. Don Francisco was as white as paper. Franz was red as a turkey-cock.

Everybody looked. Nobody spoke.

Curiously enough it was Mrs. Milhorne who found the something to say which everyone had been searching for.

" Why," she said, " whatever has been going on? "

The right question after all. Franz answered.

" I have been having with Don Francisco a little fun, *liebling*," he said. " A little game, we have."

Don Francisco looked at him.

He said nothing.

" Well," said Margherita Clarone, " I thought it was another murder."

She laughed.

" You must not be so rough, my poor Franz," she said.

" And you, Don Francisco," Jean-Artaban said, briskly jumping into such a promising fray, " you must learn not to go in for these horseplays."

Don Francisco glared at him.

" Well," said Alice, " I guess one or the other of you should have had more consideration for our nerves. I really did think something pretty awful had happened again."

Don Francisco bowed to her miserably.

"Dear madam," he said, "to-day is everything go wrong. In my offices I cannot getting. The polices are always the most questioning. And now this."

He glared at Franz.

Franz glared back.

It looked as if things might begin again.

But Don Francisco's self-pity was too overwhelming.

"It is so unfairy," he said. "Without my offices I cannot working and my brain goes roundy and roundy. And all the time comes the polices with their questioning."

"Well, that certainly is a bit hard," Alice said. "Because if I understand it right, you aren't really caught up in all this. I mean, you were out front, weren't you, where you couldn't get at the weights?"

"Yes," said Don Francisco, "it is the most unfairy."

"But why do they keep questioning you then?" Alice asked. "If they're making a nuisance of themselves someone ought to protest."

Don Francisco shrugged.

"They always want to know if I am going through the pass door," he said.

"Ah," said Jean-Artaban, "that is acute of the superintendent. It would certainly have been possible after all for you to have done that."

He stepped forward and towered over Don Francisco.

"Did you try to kill me then?" he said.

Don Francisco opened his mouth twice.

"Well," said Jean-Artaban, "did you come through the pass door and kill me?"

" You are not kill."

This feeble bleat of defiance was exactly what Jean-Artaban liked. He pounced.

" No," he said, " I am not killed. But that poor little creature is. You sacrificed her, Don Francisco, to your ruthless egoism. You killed her with as little thought as you would kill a sparrow out hunting."

" But no. No, no, no. I say no. No. No. No. No. No. It is not so. No. No. No. No. No. No."

Don Francisco had found his tongue.

" I prove her," he said, a little more articulately, " I was all the timing in front of the house. I could not have touch the weights. No, no, no, no, no, no, no, no."

He shook up and down so spasmodically over this stream of denial that even Jean-Artaban was reduced to silence.

Standing at the extreme edge of the stage away from the rest of the group Mrs. Milhorne turned to Mrs. Craggs for explanation.

" I can't see why anyone should ever think he did it," she said. " Isn't it just as he keeps saying? He was out in the front. Everybody must have been able to see him."

" Oh, no," said Mrs. Craggs. " I know he was in full view, but if you ask me no one saw him at all."

This last remark fell just in the pause that followed Don Francisco's final spate of indignant negatives.

Everybody turned in the direction of the two cleaners. Mrs. Milhorne looked abashed. Mrs. Craggs retained her customary rather dour expression beneath her forbiddingly square hat.

" Well," said Alice, " I think she's got something there."

She smiled in a friendly way at Don Francisco.

" I must say I certainly wouldn't have known if you'd come backstage," she said.

Don Francisco looked at her.

" But you were in your husband's rooming," he said. " Of course you not see me."

" Well," said Alice, " could anybody else? Could you from up on the catwalk, Jean-Artaban? "

" All I was doing was watching the stage to step at the last moment into that danger," said Jean-Artaban.

Alice looked round.

All the others who had been in the theatre when the car crashed down were there.

" All right," she said, " Franz, you were in your dressing-room, weren't you? "

" But of course, *liebling*."

" And Margherita, dear, you were in yours? "

" Certainly I was."

" Madame Glistanova, could you see through any gap in the scenery out into the auditorium? "

Xaria Glistanova shook her head.

" Now, you Mr. Einfalt," Alice went on, " where exactly were you? "

Mrs. Craggs looked quickly at Mrs. Milhorne and then turned her whole attention on to Heinrich Einfalt.

He smiled. A little uneasily.

Mrs. Craggs held her breath.

" Well," Heinrich Einfalt said, " I tell you what happened. I felt a need, you understand, to go to the lavatory. And so for a moment I deserted my wife."

He looked round at the circle of intent faces.

He half-smiled.

" But I found the place in the stage-door corridor had
been locked up. So I remembered that only round the
corner is the Dog and Seaweed pub. I walked quickly
round there, and came back just to hear the noise of the
car falling."

Mrs. Craggs looked at Mrs. Milhorne again.

" All right," said Alice, " now who else might have
seen our friend, Don Francisco? I think we ought to get
this cleared up. If he's under suspicion unjustly I intend
to go and see that Superintendent Pryde about it right
now."

She looked round the group again.

" Well, Clarissa," she said, " we ought to include you,
I guess."

Clarissa, who had been very silent after her encounter
with Franz, licked her lips slightly. She looked less
beautiful than usual.

" I didn't see Don Francisco, if that's what you want to
know," she said.

" It's not all we want to know, but I guess it's all we'll
hear," said Alice.

She turned her attention to the two cleaners.

" Well, now, ladies," she said, " can either of you help
us? "

" I'm sure I can't," Mrs. Milhorne answered quickly.
" I was as much in the dressing-room I was doing over as
any of the singers was in theirs."

" Quite right, dear," Alice said.

"And the same goes for me," said Mrs. Craggs. " But
I don't know why you should be asking me, I'm sure.
There's only one person who's really likely to have seen
Don Francisco. And that's you, Monsieur Paul."

Paul looked back at them stupidly.

" Well," said Alice, " did you see Don Francisco sitting in the stalls at the time of the murder? "

" But of course not," Paul said sulkily. " Everybody knows that the orchestra pit is always too deep to be able to see out of it."

Abruptly attention left him.

It concentrated on Don Francisco.

" Well," said Jean-Artaban, " I regret to say, my dear friend, we shall have to include you in the list of active suspects. And personally I put you pretty high."

CHAPTER XIX

To THIS COLLECTIVE indictment Don Francisco replied with silence. The streams of protests seemed to have dried up entirely.

For a little while it even looked as if he was about to confess.

Mrs. Craggs broke the long pause.

" Of course," she said, " what's been said doesn't really help all that much. It just means that someone who most people thought had got an alibi hasn't after all."

Don Francisco looked across at her with pathetic gratitude.

Like a dog.

Mrs. Craggs sniffed.

" We've already had to add Miss Glass to the list," she said. " And it won't be the last."

She collected a chorus of startled glances.

"Well, *liebling*," Franz said, "you seem to be very sure of yourself. Why do you say that?"

Mrs. Craggs was by no means awed.

"Because it's true," she replied matter-of-factly.

"But how do you know it's true, *liebling*?"

Mrs. Craggs smiled a little grimly.

"I can show you easily enough," she said.

"I certainly think you should speak up, and at once," Xaria Glistanova said.

"Well, then, I will," said Mrs. Craggs. "After all, what I've got to say is no more than anybody could think out for themselves. I've no doubt Superintendent Pryde has done. That's why he kept asking Don Francisco so many questions. He knew that people were wrong when they said he was out of the running."

"All right, then," Margherita broke in, "who else is in the running?"

"Monsieur Paul, of course," Mrs. Craggs said.

Once more Paul was the centre of attention.

He stood looking awkwardly at the neutral-coloured surface of the stage and swinging his large-fisted hands in an ungainly way to and fro.

"It's quite simple," Mrs. Craggs went on, "he's just said he was too far down in the orchestra pit to see Don Francisco. Well, the opposite applies. No one could see him."

"Oh, *liebling*," Franz burst out, "you must not set up as a detective. You make such huge mistakes, *liebling*. It is funny."

He giggled.

Mrs. Craggs looked stern under her stern hat.

" Well," Alice said, " put us out of our misery like a good boy, Franz. What mistake has she made? "

Franz brought his giggles to an end with difficulty.

" The music," he gasped. " The music."

" Ah, I see," said Alice.

She turned to Mrs. Craggs.

" It looks as if you've given poor Paul an unnecessary scare," she said. " After all he was playing the music for the scene when Mary Arthur was killed. I suppose you're not suggesting he managed to transfer it to a tape recorder or something? I guess with a load of trained musicians in the place no one could possibly get away with that. The quality would show it up at once."

" A load of trained musicians."

Xaria Glistanova repeated the phrase contemptuously.

" Mrs. Craggs is right," she went on, " and the load of trained musicians doesn't seem to have seen why."

" Well, why then? " Alice said.

" Because there's no accompaniment just at that time of the opera," Mrs. Craggs answered. " I can hear it now, the lovely voice of that kid floating out all by itself into the dark. And then that crash."

It was plain to see from the faces of the others that they, too, remembered now. It was not a pleasant memory.

" Yes," said Alice slowly, " that's quite true. It does look as if Paul is added to the list. That makes the full twelve now, or eleven if the idea was to kill you, Jean-Artaban."

She looked at her husband.

The anxiety spelt out for all to see.

" It may be more than eleven," said Mrs. Craggs.

" More? How can it be? " Madame Glistanova said sharply.

" It has to be," Mrs. Craggs replied.

She seemed in no way abashed to be laying down the law in this fashion.

" Hasn't anybody asked themselves," she went on, " how Mr. Einfalt got out of the theatre and Miss Glass got in? "

" Well, yes, I did," Mrs. Milhorne said wonderingly.

Alice looked up again.

" And how was it? " she said.

" They walked past Mr. Strutt," said Mrs. Craggs. " I knew all along he wasn't the watchdog he made himself out to be. But if the police were satisfied, I wasn't going to say anything."

" But you are going to now? " Alice said with a touch of sharpness.

" Well, I've been proved right now, haven't I? I thought Mr. Strutt was dozing in his box when I went to get the police. Otherwise he'd have come when he heard the crash, wouldn't he? I'll give him watchdog."

Her eyes gleamed with satisfaction.

" Then it could have been anyone who committed the crime," Alice said slowly.

She sounded relieved, and a little apprehensive.

But Mrs. Craggs had not finished.

" That's what I thought first go off," she said. " But when you come to think about it proper you see it's got to be someone who knew what was going on. It stands to reason. There weren't many moments when anyone could have got at those weights without being seen. No, I still think it must have been one of us."

They looked round at each other.

::   ::

When Mrs. Craggs was dusting Jean-Artaban's dressing-room that afternoon the door was briskly opened and Jean-Artaban's wife put her head round the corner.

" Oh," she said. " Oh, hallo there. I was looking for my husband. With this wonderful weather going on and no rehearsal I want to get out into the countryside all I can. You should see some of the woods around the town : just one single mass of deep gold to see. They really are magnificent."

" You want to see 'em while you can," Mrs. Craggs said. " You never know with the weather this time of year. There's only got to be a gale get up and in one night the trees'll be as bare as charity."

" I guess so," Alice said. " But even if you haven't seen my husband I don't know what to do. I've looked every place else I can think of."

" No," said Mrs. Craggs, " I haven't seen hair nor hide of him this afternoon."

Alice sighed.

She looked round the dressing-room at a loss.

Jean-Artaban's big fur-collared overcoat was hanging on the back of the door.

" I guess if he's left his coat he can't be far away," she said.

She lifted from a chair the ornate turban of rich silk which Jean-Artaban wore as Osmin in *Il Seraglio* and sat down. With some despondency she stared at her reflection in the big mirror surrounded by electric-light bulbs. She did not seem altogether pleased with what she saw.

Suddenly she turned to Mrs. Craggs.

" Tell me frankly, dear," she said, " I look a wreck, don't I? "

Mrs. Craggs did not stop her dusting.

" You look very nice, madam," she replied.

Alice looked at her sharply in the mirror.

" Well," she said, " you didn't bother any too much to make that convincing. You didn't even look at me."

" I didn't need to," Mrs. Craggs said. " I know you get all the help you want from hairdressers and manicurists and what not, you couldn't help but look nice."

" Well, I guess in a way that's true."

Alice leant forward in her chair and stared intently into the mirror.

" But all the same," she said, " I don't think the result is so good."

She turned to Mrs. Craggs.

" I worry about it, dear," she said. " I have that husband of mine to hold. And there's always so many pretty girls around in a theatre."

" Most of them in this theatre are better to hear than to look at," Mrs. Craggs said.

" Well, I have to agree with you there. Except for some of them. Like that Clarissa Glass."

In the big square mirror Alice caught the quick, quickly suppressed, movement of Mrs. Craggs's head.

" Oh," she said, " she is beautiful, dear. Really beautiful. I can't see anything to stop Jean-Artaban going back to her."

" I can," said Mrs. Craggs.

" What, dear? "

Mrs. Craggs's mouth set in a firm line.

"What your husband did to her in *Tosca*," she said. "She may be a beauty, but she's a singer, too. And she won't forgive him for that. Ever."

Alice sighed.

"Yes," she said, "I suppose you're right. That certainly was a terrible thing to do. I never thought Jean-Artaban would go as far as that."

She looked round at Mrs. Craggs again.

"You know, dear," she said, "when I first heard about it it made me feel quite ill. I just had to sit down right where I was till I felt better."

"Yes," said Mrs. Craggs, "I remember. You went all over white. I wondered about it at the time."

Alice smiled.

"I guess I know what you wondered, too," she said. "I thought about it afterwards. You wondered if I wasn't just discovering that I'd tried to kill Jean-Artaban for no good reason. No one had told me that he'd done that to Clarissa. I might have thought he was still in love with her. And if I'd tried to kill him I would have killed the wrong person and all for nothing. I should have gone white all right."

Alice tried a slight adjustment of her blued hair in the mirror.

"I'd leave it alone, dear, if I were you," Mrs. Craggs said.

Alice looked again.

"I guess you're right," she said.

But she continued to stare at her reflection.

"No," she said, "I decided long ago that I didn't mind about affairs like the Clarissa episode. Well, not for myself anyway. Not as a woman."

" But you minded in some other ways," Mrs. Craggs suggested.

Alice said nothing.

" You minded for your family, your name, was it? " Mrs. Craggs said.

Alice turned from the big mirror.

" Yes," she said, " yes, I did. I hated the thought that anyone would think a Towell had made a bad bargain."

The note of faint wonder in her voice.

" And now," she added, " I think I've even gotten over that. All this horrible business has at least had that good effect on me."

She sat up a little straighter.

" Though, mind you," she said, " I made him put an end to the Clarissa business as soon as I heard of it, I just told him that if he wanted his little extra financial supplies he'd got to behave."

Again she drooped.

" I wish he hadn't done what I wanted in such a damned brutal way," she said. " Still, I guess it was his way of hitting back. And he hit all right."

She relapsed into silence.

Mrs. Craggs finished her dusting.

" Well," she said, " I must be off now then."

" Yeah. Well, thanks for listening to me. And if you do come across that husband of mine, tell him I'm waiting for him here."

As Mrs. Craggs closed the door Alice added a last instruction.

" And say I'm getting just a little mad," she called.

But when Mrs. Craggs did find Jean-Artaban she realised at once that it was not the time to deliver any messages, even suitably edited. It was plain that Jean-Artaban would not want anyone to know what he was doing.

He was in earnest conversation with Franz.

Mrs. Craggs caught the sound of two quiet but intense voices as she went near the entrance to the scene dock on her way across to the ladies' side dressing-rooms.

It was Jean-Artaban she heard first.

" I tell you," he was saying, " I must have another hundred pounds, at once, to-day."

" But I can't go on giving you money all the time," Franz replied. " It was only yesterday you had the last lot."

" I don't see why that means I can't have more to-day."

" But it's ridiculous. You boast to my face how much you make from your singing and then you come and ask to borrow a hundred pounds when you have no intention of paying it back."

" That at least is quite right," Jean-Artaban said.

" But why do you do it, *liebling*? Why? "

" You know very well why. I have certain expenses that I do not wish to discuss with my wife."

" But if you make so much yourself? "

" I also spend a great deal myself. Please do not think you are the only singer in the world who is well paid."

" Well," Franz answered, " all the same I do not see why, if you make so much money, you need to borrow from me."

" Do you want me to tell you why? "

Mrs. Craggs, frankly eavesdropping, manœuvred herself carefully until she could see into the scene dock without being seen.

Standing close to each other surrounded on both sides by great stacked tall flats Jean-Artaban and Franz were staring intently at one another. As if each was determined not to lower his eyes come what might.

" Do you want me to tell you why? " Jean-Artaban repeated.

Mrs. Craggs could see Franz lick his lips.

" No? " said Jean-Artaban. " Then I will give myself that little pleasure."

He leant forward over the tubby Austrian.

" I will tell you why," he said. " Because when I was singing as a guest at the Vienna State Opera I amused myself with a little research. And in the course of it I discovered on what day of what year a certain Franz Prahler had been born."

Mrs. Craggs saw him smile.

" And that year, my dear Franz," he concluded, " was a very, very long time ago."

And now Franz lowered his eyes.

" So," said Jean-Artaban more briskly, " if you want in this absurdly vain manner to conceal from the world that you are really rather an old man—— "

" No."

" Oh, come, don't let there be polite evasions between such old friends. It would be ridiculous to talk about you as ' such a late middle-aged man ', let us—— "

" But that is the truth. The real truth."

Jean-Artaban smiled again.

" I prefer to state that you are old," he said. " You are old and vain, and will make out a cheque for one hundred English pounds at once."

Franz took a cheque book from the pocket of his short

tweed jacket. He turned and laid it out among the paint pots on a rough wooden table nearby. And he signed.

CHAPTER XX

THE NOTORIETY that the murder had brought to the Flinwich Festival had at least had the effect of ensuring full houses for the rest of the season. Mrs. Craggs and Mrs. Milhorne had had to find themselves somewhere to sit in a remote corner of the wings to hear that evening's performance of *Il Seraglio* instead of being able to loll in empty seats in the back stalls, as they had done for the memorable *Tosca* which ended with Baron Scarpia alive and triumphing. They were now squashed not at all happily into the golden throne pushed away near the entrance to the stage-door corridor.

The throne had been designed on an impressive scale, but it held the two cleaners side by side only with the greatest difficulty. And they could see nothing of what was going on on the stage. To Mrs. Craggs, who knew her Mozart, this was not a great deprivation. But it did mean that, even more than with the operas they had watched from the auditorium, she was constantly distracted by the many questions of Mrs. Milhorne.

And to-night they seemed even more pressing than was warranted by the backstage view of the opera. Not only did Mrs. Milhorne demand to know at every instant what was supposed to be going on on the stage, showing all the while her customary lack of intellectual grasp of the plot, but she also required information on a whole host of technical points.

The veteran singer who was playing the second tenor role of the servant Pedrillo had only to pause before going on stage to have a generous spit and Mrs. Milhorne was off.

" What did he do that for? "

" A lot of singers do it."

" Do they? Ladies as well as gentlemen? "

Mrs. Craggs sighed.

" Probably not the ladies, certainly not ones that has a right to call themselves ladies."

" But why did he do it anyhow? "

" To clear his throat, of course."

" So that he can sing better? "

" What else? "

" Then what happens if you don't do it? Does it make you sing worse? "

Mrs. Craggs listened with pantomime intentness to Jean-Artaban raging with musical fury in the part of Osmin.

But Mrs. Milhorne was taking no hints.

" Isn't it a bad thing not to have a good spit? " she whispered with redoubled hissing.

Mrs. Craggs turned to her briefly.

" The others manage some different way," she said. " You can always take out a handkerchief or something, can't you? "

" Oh, yes, so you could," Mrs. Milhorne answered. " I'm glad about that."

A little later they watched Franz prepare in his fashion

to make his second appearance of the evening in the part of the hero, Belmonte. He further increased Mrs. Milhorne's inquisitiveness by giving his forehead a vigorous tapping just above the bridge of the nose.

" Does everybody do that? " Mrs. Milhorne immediately wanted to know.

" No, not everybody."

But this was by no means enough to put Mrs. Milhorne off.

" Who then? " she whispered.

Mrs. Craggs's eyes blazed like two indignant coals of fire.

" The ones that believe it helps," she answered.

" But why do they believe it helps? "

" I don't know. I think they believe it draws the resonance into the hollow part just inside your head."

" Is there a hollow there really? "

Mrs. Craggs bent all her attention on Franz singing " *O wie ängstlich, o wie feuerig.*" This was not difficult because he was singing the romantic outpouring with a rare golden beauty.

When the aria had ended Mrs. Craggs sank back a little in the uncomfortable throne. A slight movement caught her eye.

Mrs. Milhorne was busy tapping her forehead just above the bridge of the nose.

Even the interval did not release Mrs. Craggs.

" I tell you something," Mrs. Milhorne said as they strolled up and down the grimy street outside the stage door easing their cramped limbs. " I'll tell you something very funny."

" Yes? "

" Do you know what I saw in Clarissa Glass's dressing-room just before she came to dress this evening? "

" What were you doing in there? "

" I was looking for a duster which I happened to have mislaid."

Mrs. Milhorne sounded offended.

" It was a new one," she added. " Nice and fluffy. I didn't like to see it go."

" You should keep your hands on your dusters. Then you wouldn't lose them. That's the second this week."

" Well, we can't all be thinking of things like dusters all the time. Some of us have got minds above the sordid level of life."

" Oh, yes? "

A short silence.

" Well, as I was saying," Mrs. Milhorne resumed on the confidential note that had somehow got lost, " what do you think she had in her dressing-room? "

" I don't know. How should I? "

" Then I'll tell you. There was two eggs, raw. In a glass. And that wasn't all."

A horrified pause.

" No, what else was there then? " Mrs. Craggs said. " A man? I wouldn't be surprised at that, I can tell you."

" It was nothing like that at all."

Mrs. Milhorne was plainly deciding whether it was worth pursuing a conversation with someone of such irredeemably low tastes as her friend, Mrs. Craggs. Eventually the desire for enlightenment got the better of her.

Not for the first time.

" No," she said, " it was nothing of that sort at all. It

was a saucer with two prunes on it. Uncooked prunes, mind. You don't think she was going to eat them, do you? "

" 'Course she was."

" For the good of her voice? "

" Yes. It's quite a common thing to do."

" And the eggs? "

" Yes, she was going to eat them, too. Swallow them down."

" Raw? Just like that? "

" Yes, of course."

" Oh, I see."

Mrs. Milhorne relapsed into a profound meditation which lasted until well into the next act. It was in fact only the strong impact of a curt conversation that took place within a few feet of the golden throne that brought her to life again.

The participants were Jean-Artaban and the soprano playing Blonde, the English maid.

The conversation was short.

But pointed.

The Blonde began it.

" If you ever do that again to me," she said, " I'll slap your face."

Jean-Artaban raised his eyebrows.

" Do what? " he asked. " Sing better than you? "

" You know quite well what : upstage me. How the heck can I make myself heard over your great roaring voice when I'm miles upstaged? "

Jean-Artaban smiled.

" My dear young lady," he said, " it is my privilege to sing from whatever place on the stage I choose. I wouldn't try to deprive me of it if I were you. Worse things could happen to you, much worse."

He swung round and strode off in the direction of the men's dressing-rooms.

Mrs. Milhorne nudged Mrs. Craggs.

On the stage Clarissa was making a very fair attempt at the depths of feeling in " *Trauigkeit ward mir zum Loose*." But Mrs. Craggs, who treasured memories of Salzburg productions on the wireless, was content to let it go by.

" Well? " she said.

" Upstaging," said Mrs. Milhorne. " What's it mean? "

" Don't you keep your ears open for five minutes round the theatre? It means going further upstage from the person you're playing with so that if they want to appear to be singing to you they have to turn and sing away from the audience."

Mrs. Milhorne worked it out.

" But it's a downright dirty trick," she said.

" Of course it is. If you're fool enough to fall for it."

" But you have to, don't you? I mean, you couldn't just catch hold of the person and keep them where you wanted them to be, could you? "

Mrs. Craggs smiled grimly.

" Stranger things have happened in opera," she said.

" But that's not what you do do? "

" No," said Mrs. Craggs.

She gave a curt laugh.

" What you do is quite simple," she said. " You ignore the other singer altogether. You just turn and face the audience and give 'em all you've got. After all, opera's never very lifelike at best, is it? "

" No, I suppose not."

Mrs. Milhorne reflected.

Mrs. Craggs allowed Clarissa's performance to revive memories of better ones.

" There's a lot of snags to it, that's certain," Mrs. Milhorne summed up. " There's no doubt you'd need your head screwed on all right. Perhaps that was what was wrong with that poor little Mary Arthur. After all, she was only a kid."

Mrs. Craggs turned sharply in the constricting golden throne.

" What was wrong? " she said.

" Her being too young."

" I know that. But why did it make a difference? "

She put the question without politeness.

Mrs. Milhorne was slow to come to terms with it.

" Oh," she said at last, " because of that row I heard them having, in the scene dock, you know. Didn't I tell you about it? "

" Of course you did. That's why I asked you what you meant just now. A sort of idea came into my head."

" Did it, dear? "

Mrs. Milhorne looked at her.

" Now, listen to me," said Mrs. Craggs, " what exactly was that row about? "

This time Mrs. Milhorne answered without hesitation.

" But I told you," she said, " about upstaging."

Mrs. Craggs smiled.

Like a crocodile that has just dealt with an agreeably tender monkey.

" Let me get it quite straight," she said. " The row you overheard between Jean-Artaban and Mary Arthur in the scene dock was about him upstaging her. And she threatened that if he ever did it again she would make him pay? "

" Yes, that's right. Just like the girl did just now, only she was more Australian about it, if you take my meaning."

Mrs. Milhorne was patient.

" And it was only because you didn't know what up-staging was that you put two and two together and made it out that Jean-Artaban had tried to rape her? " Mrs. Craggs asked.

Mrs. Milhorne looked shocked.

" I'm sure I never let a word like that through my lips," she said.

" No," said Mrs. Craggs, " you didn't, dear. Not the word. Only the idea."

Her face was grim as a Fury's.

" Yes," she said at last, " that means there's only one possible explanation. Now we'll see if he gets on to it."

" If who gets—— "

Mrs. Milhorne's inquiry was abruptly terminated.

On stage the action had reached that difficult point for the producer when the Pasha Selim has for the umpteenth time urged his suit on the unfortunate captive heroine Constanze, and before she launches into her definitive repudiation " *Martern aller Arten* " the long orchestral introduction has to be played. Hitherto Don Francisco had let the Pasha and Clarissa glare at each other in the traditional way until the time arrived for Clarissa to draw a merciful breath and launch into the aria.

But earlier in the day, as he had padded restlessly about the theatre longing to get back to his office, an idea had struck him. The great awkward pause would provide a splendid opportunity to justify the presence on Mr. Strutt's allotment of four clamorous peacocks. They could be released into the Pasha's garden, where their presence was entirely plausible, at precisely this difficult point. Then the audience would look at them instead of having to be content with staring at the two stationary stage figures.

It was the sight of Mr. Strutt staggering past with two peacocks hanging by their legs from either hand that had frozen Mrs. Milhorne to silence.

Mr. Strutt strode towards the Pasha's garden. Don Francisco darted forward and barred his way. The Pasha was still urging his suit.

The peacocks struggled like tormented demons.

Mr. Strutt went four shades redder than his customary angry puce.

" I can't hold 'em, sir," he grunted. " I can't hold 'em."

He made little attempt to keep his voice down.

" One momenting, one momenting more," Don Francisco begged.

He turned to the stage and sent out a complex and energetic gesture towards the Pasha indicating that he should speed his wooing.

Plainly the Pasha did not understand.

The peacocks fluttered even more furiously.

Mr. Strutt fixed his popping eyes on the stage and took a pace forward.

Don Francisco held his arms wide.

And mercifully from behind him he heard the Pasha conclude his arguments.

He nipped nimbly out of the way.

Mr. Strutt hurled the first handful of peacocks into the air. They sailed forward on to the stage in a wild whirl of wings and tails. Into the existing confusion Mr. Strutt hastily catapulted the second handful of peacocks. The consequent outbreaking of frenzied squawking scarcely contributed to Boscani's delicate phrasing of the introduction to " *Martern aller Arten*."

Three long peacock tail-feathers floated out into the auditorium.

The birds settled on the stage.

They looked rumpled, spiteful and not in the least beautiful. Clarissa backed away from them.

The full-scale orchestral introduction steadied in its stride again.

And the most ruffled of the peacocks lifted up its elegant neck and let out at full force its characteristic cry.

The orchestra stopped.

The appallingly strident sound made music a total impossibility.

Clarissa looked at the Pasha. The Pasha looked at Clarissa. The other three peacocks joined in the cry.

Clarissa and the Pasha jointly rushed towards them brandishing their arms, hissing, and kicking out with their legs. Although they were fated never to marry, it was plain that they had a good deal in common. It might have made for a happy united existence, especially if peacocks continued to be prevalent in that part of Turkey.

Their joint efforts were at length successful. The peacocks suddenly could stand it no longer, they turned tail and fled.

Down in the orchestra pit Boscani opened his eyes again and signalled to the musicians. The introduction to

" *Martern aller Arten* " began again. The Pasha and his
fair captive resumed their positions opposite each other,
and glared.

From behind the scenery faint bumps and bangs could
be heard as Mr. Strutt set about recapturing the peacocks
before taking them once again back to his allotment.

The opera resumed its course. On the whole the
standard of performance was not bad. Jean-Artaban,
though vocally not the best possible Osmin, delighted in
the part as a part. Mrs. Craggs looked forward to his final
gloating " *Ha, wie will ich triumphieren,*" for which he was
well provided both with easy top E and bottom D and the
right vengefully unpleasant psychological approach.

Clarissa, too, made a reasonable Constanze. If she was
really just a little too weak vocally, her forceful beauty
helped to overcome much of the deficiency and her statuesque acting was for once no grave disadvantage. And
opposite her Franz was, of course, a superb Belmonte.
This was one of the parts for which he was famous all over
the world. Down in the orchestra pit Boscani was now
coaxing and wheedling splendid playing from the
orchestra and the subsidiary singers were of excellent
standard. Altogether it was a performance Mrs. Craggs
was glad to be hearing.

So it was all the more annoying when further interrup-
tions began to make themselves felt.

They manifested themselves at first by renewed backstage activity. Don Francisco, disembarrassed of the peacocks, still kept hurrying to and fro, although he at least
moved discreetly. The same could not be said for Superintendent Pryde and Sergeant Jenkins.

It became apparent for the first time that the sergeant

wore police boots with his plain inconspicuous everyday suit. And they creaked.

Neither superintendent nor sergeant seemed to be able to whisper quietly. They held three separate little conferences with Don Francisco standing in the darkness of the wings, and although Mrs. Craggs could hear nothing but the shushing and spluttering, it made listening to the music an impossibility.

She turned to Mrs. Milhorne.

" Come on," she said, " I'm going to nip round out of the stage door and in through the foyer. I'd rather stand at the back than have that noise going on."

" Yes," said Mrs. Milhorne, " I think I ought to see it from the front as well as from the back."

They set off quickly.

Mr. Strutt, sitting in his cubicle with four peacocks hanging upside down from the ceiling above him, was much too exhausted to delay them. There was no one in the foyer and they were able to walk quickly through and quietly pull open the door leading to the back of the stalls.

They were just in time.

As they turned to the stage the Pedrillo had just begun his serenade " *Im Mohrenland gefangen war*," the signal to Belmonte and Constanze that all is safe for them to escape. Mrs. Craggs watched as Clarissa negotiated the ladder down from the upper window of the Pasha's house.

Mrs. Milhorne sighed with heavy relief as she at last reached the ground and stole safely away to the waiting boat and freedom.

The mute guard was duly woken by the signal serenade and in accordance with the libretto duly left the stage to summon Osmin to help him foil the escape and to send guards to the boat to seize the first eloping pair.

But when Constanze was brought back to confront the furious Osmin, and just as Mrs. Craggs was settling down to enjoy Jean-Artaban's " *Ha, wie will ich triumphieren,*" she appeared, not surrounded by the Pasha's guards, but in very different circumstances.

CHAPTER XXI

CLARISSA WAS ESCORTED by none other than Pryde of the Yard and his faithful Sergeant Jenkins.

They led her briskly on to the stage, each looking intently serious.

Suddenly the contrast between the mysterious half-darkness behind the set and the penetrating light on the stage impinged on them.

They looked all round in a puzzled way.

Only several seconds later did it occur to them, all too plainly, that the black wall in front of them was the auditorium. And that it was filled by five or six hundred perplexed, astounded and delighted opera-goers.

"Jenkins, this is the bloody stage."

Superintendent Pryde's voice carried well even to the very back of the gallery.

The two policemen, still grasping the frightened-looking Clarissa, turned.

They looked for refuge.

The Oriental complexity of the scenery seemed to baffle them.

They entered the Pasha's garden and made for the steps

of his house. Then suddenly they seemed to doubt whether such an unlikely-looking door could possibly lead anywhere.

They swept round.

And this time the low walls of the Pasha's garden appeared to constitute an insurmountable obstacle. The two men obviously could not believe that it was unnecessary to negotiate the entrance to the garden in order to get out. Ignoring the wide gap between two flats at the edge of the stage they plunged towards the little ornamental ironwork garden gate.

Both superintendent and sergeant tried to go through it at the same time, and each hung grimly on to Clarissa between them. A hopeless jam developed.

" Go back, man," Superintendent Pryde roared. " The way we came in."

With all the quickness of decision that had sent him up the ladder of promotion at Scotland Yard he wheeled and ran, dragging Clarissa with him.

There was a final slight contretemps when they came up against the delightfully fantasticated boat at the bottom of the Pasha's garden. The superintendent smartly pushed Clarissa forward. For a single moment they stood poised on the vessel's prow till Pryde of the Yard gave Clarissa an uncompromising shove and they vanished from view.

Left on the stage Sergeant Jenkins suddenly understood about the gap between the flats. He dived gratefully through it.

" I'll be seeing you," Mrs. Craggs said quickly to Mrs. Milhorne.

" Why? Where are you going? "

But she had not stopped to answer.

She hurried out before any of the startled opera-goers had begun to leave and went at a trotting run along the bleak street to the stage door.

She was just in time.

Superintendent Pryde was hurrying down the stage-door corridor clutching Clarissa by the elbow.

Puffing awkwardly and with her face blotched with colour Mrs. Craggs barred his way.

" Wait," she said.

The superintendent looked at her.

" Are you arresting Miss Glass? " Mrs. Craggs managed to ask.

The words were in the form of a question. But they were an accusation.

" Now then," Superintendent Pryde said, " I'm in a very great hurry so please stand out of the way."

He advanced down the corridor still gripping Clarissa's elbow.

Mrs. Craggs stood firm.

" I suppose you think she tried to kill Monsieur Pivoine? " she said.

" Will you get out of my way? "

" That's what you believe, isn't it? " Mrs. Craggs said.

She fired the question at the superintendent with the violence of a pistol shot.

" What if it is? Stand aside."

This final bafflement in a series of humiliations was too much for the superintendent's temper.

" You've got it all wrong," said Mrs. Craggs. " You'll let the real culprit get clear away."

" I make no mistakes."

The superintendent's large-featured face was dull red

with rage. His great black eyebrows were hooked fiercely together.

"Oh, yes, you do make mistakes. Listen. Did you know that Monsieur Pivoine had told everybody he never got into the god's car till the last second. Did you know that?"

"Move aside or I'll have you arrested."

Mrs. Craggs's dumpy body stayed unyieldingly put.

And from behind the superintendent came the answer to her question. From Jean-Artaban himself, still garishly resplendent in the turban and baggy trousers of Osmin.

"Yes," he said, "of course the superintendent knew. I told him myself."

Mrs. Craggs looked at Pryde of the Yard.

The expression on her face was unmistakable.

Contempt.

"And you still believe the idea was to kill Monsieur Pivoine?" she said. "If the murderer knew that, they'd have been bound to look up to see if he was in the car before they tipped the weights off. They didn't do that, so it means only one thing. They wanted to kill Mary Arthur."

The superintendent's grip on Clarissa's elbow slackened.

Mrs. Craggs pressed home her advantage.

"And there's only one person who could have wanted to kill Mary Arthur," she said.

Cautiously Pryde of the Yard let go of Clarissa's arm. She continued to stand where she was, looking all the more beautiful for being ruffled and unsure of herself. In front of her stood Mrs. Craggs, stumpy and implacable. Behind her loomed Jean-Artaban, too curious to dream of moving.

" You see at once," Mrs. Craggs went on, " that it couldn't have been Miss Glass here. What would she want with Mary Arthur? Her only concern was Monsieur Pivoine. That was why she crept into the theatre that night : to avoid seeing him."

" Well, you're right about that anyhow," Clarissa murmured.

" In fact," Mrs. Craggs continued, " Miss Glass hardly knew Mary Arthur. And that goes for some of the others, too, Madame Pivoine, young Albert Sime, Mrs. Milhorne, myself if it comes to that. You'd have to be pretty desperate to want to make out a case against us."

" That's an attitude I confess I shared all along."

From behind the massive bulk of Jean-Artaban came the cool New England voice of his wife.

" And some of the others had good reason for wanting her to stay alive," Mrs. Craggs said. " Don Francisco did and so did Herr Prahler."

" My dear."

It was Xaria Glistanova, also lost somewhere behind the gigantic Jean-Artaban.

" My dear, you should be careful. You are eliminating each of us in turn. Soon there will be only one left. You are doing a dangerous thing."

" I'm saying who killed Mary Arthur," Mrs. Craggs replied.

She did not take her eyes off Superintendent Pryde.

" So," she said, " who next? Monsieur Paul? Well, he loved her. I'm sorry to have to say that out loud, but it's true and anyone with half an eye in their head could see it. He wept when she died."

Mrs. Craggs straightened her back a little.

" There is one person who might be thought to have a reason for wanting to end Mary Arthur's life," she said. " The only person in the world who has ever sung the Goose Girl. That was going to be taken away from her, and everyone knows the lengths vanity will take a singer to."

Xaria Glistanova interrupted her.

" I warned you you were being foolish," she said.

" Yes," said Mrs. Craggs, " I would have been foolish if I had thought you of all people had killed out of vanity. Anyone can see you're the least vain person in the world."

She glanced at the towering bulk of Jean-Artaban.

" Unlike someone I could name," she said, " who was so vain that he refused to admit he'd been bested in a silly row about upstaging by a chit of a girl. That was all the contact Monsieur Pivoine had with Mary Arthur."

" Then who—— " Alice began to ask.

" It leaves one person," said Mrs. Craggs. " The one person who had the same reason for wanting to end Mary Arthur's life as Madame Glistanova. Her husband. The one she had scorned three kings to marry. The one who had so little pride in himself that you didn't want to look at him, and who had the pride of madness for his wife. No, not even for his wife. For his wife's voice."

Under her square-set hat Mrs. Craggs's face was uncompromising.

" He even tried to do it before," she said. " Remember he was at Dallas when Madame Da Costa-O'Brien was to sing the Goose Girl and trouble over the god's car made them give up the idea."

" No. It must not be like this."

From somewhere under Jean-Artaban's rounded waist the short figure of Heinrich Einfalt shot forward.

The open stage door lay in front of him.

Outside the autumn night glittered with stars.

Heinrich Einfalt put his head down and ran.

Superintendent Pryde, Pryde of the Yard, with all the quickness which had sent him to the top of the promotion ladder, grabbed him in a grip of steel.

Sergeant Jenkins appeared from nowhere beside his chief.

" We'll take him to the station right away," the superintendent said. " It's a good thing I had a car waiting."

The small group watched the discreet dark-blue car drive quickly away.

Just as its lights disappeared round the corner, Mrs. Milhorne came up along the street. She joined Mrs. Craggs.

" I'm sorry I didn't come with you just now, dear," she said.

Mrs. Craggs turned and looked at her.

" Oh, yes? " she said.

" Yes," said Mrs. Milhorne, " but you see I'd got a lot to think about."

She turned her pale, lank, dreamy face up to the brilliant starry sky.

" I didn't tell you before," she said, " but Herr Prahler happened to hear me singing in the theatre this morning. He says I've got the most promising voice he's ever heard. He told me that one day I'll sing the Goose Girl in *Death of A Fat God*."